BENEATH THE ICY DEPTHS

BENEATH THE ICY DEPTHS

PARKS PAT MYSTERIES
BOOK TWELVE

P.D. WORKMAN

PD WORKMAN

ISBN: 9781774686607 (KDP Paperback)
ISBN: 9781774686621 (KDP Hardcover)
ISBN: 9781774686591 (Large Print)
ISBN: 9781774686614 (Lulu Paperback)
ISBN: 9781774686584 (ePub)
ISBN: 9781774686638 (Accessible Audio)

Gentle Angel

Rushin' Death

Posed for Death

Death of a Corpse

Endowed with Death

Shattered to Death

Captured in Death

Currying Death

Healed to Death

Death's Charm

Bleeding Hearts Valley Thrillers

An Abrupt Departure

High-Tech Crime Solvers Series

Virtually Harmless

Cowritten with D. D. VanDyke

California Corwin P. I. Mystery Series

The Girl in the Morgue

Stand Alone Suspense Novels

Looking Over Your Shoulder

Lion Within

Pursued by the Past

In the Tick of Time

Loose the Dogs

AND MORE AT PDWORKMAN.COM

To those fighting to take back the cold, dark nights.

STYLE NOTE

Since my largest readership is in the USA, I have chosen to use US spellings throughout this series. That includes the Americanization of centre to center, even where it is an actual place name, just for consistency's sake. I apologize to my Canadian readers for this.

I have chosen, however, to use Canadian grammar, particularly for Canadian voices. If you see what you think is a grammar error, it may just be Canadian, eh?

CHAPTER ONE

*M*argie was working at her desk. Snoozing, if she were to be honest with herself. The bullpen was warm and Margie had hit her midafternoon slump, trying to push through some paperwork but making little progress.

The phone ringing jolted her awake. She nearly fell out of her chair. She reached for the receiver, looking at the phone number on the display as she did so. The number was familiar, but she couldn't put a name to it until she picked it up and heard the voice.

"Detective Patenaude," she greeted.

"Detective Parks Pat," Gagnon's French-accented nasal voice drilled into her ear. "They're asking for you at this scene."

She knew that Gagnon had been called out to a newly discovered body an hour or two earlier. She had envied his going out, even though she didn't much feel like standing outside in the cold today. At least it was something to do.

"They're asking for me?" she repeated.

"They need your particular area of expertise."

Margie's area of expertise was nothing more than having been called out to attend a few murder scenes at Calgary parks, which had led to her being dubbed Parks Pat, and now she was the expert on bodies found in parks and wilderness areas.

She also attributed it in part to her Métis heritage. It gave her a bit of mystique, with people thinking that due to her European explorer and Indigenous Cree ancestry, she must have some special connection with nature and have learned tracking and lore at her parents' knees.

She was doing her best to learn more about Mother Earth and her secrets from Moushoom, her grandfather, but Margie had grown up a city girl and was woefully bereft of instinct in the area of tracking or even following a map. It was a standing joke how easily she could get lost, even following GPS directions.

But, despite Margie's lack of skills or specialized knowledge, she was the proclaimed expert on deaths in parks, and they would keep calling her out to the scenes of murders or accidents in Calgary parks for as long as she worked homicide in the city. There was no shaking the name and reputation now.

"We're at Bowness Park," Gagnon told her. "You know it?"

"Sure, I know Bowness Park," Margie agreed, happy she was familiar with this one. She remembered visiting Bowness Park as a child on vacations to Calgary. Most of her trips there had been during the summer, when they had enjoyed picnics and BBQs, riding the zip line, and playing tag on the other playground equipment. The couple of Christmases that she had spent in Calgary, they had gone skating on the lagoon in Bowness. There had been fires and hot chocolate, and it had been a lot of fun. Margie had enjoyed skating and had not been bothered at all by her fear of water. Frozen water held no terrors for her.

Boating during the summer was another story. But skating in the winter was a good memory. She had loved spending that time with her cousins and other members of her extended family.

"So you can get out here?" Gagnon pressed.

"Yeah, you bet. I have my car. It should take me about… half an hour to get down…" Margie hazarded a guess, even though she had no idea how long it would actually take.

"Dress warmly," Gagnon warned.

Margie had her toque, gloves, and other winter gear in the car, so that wouldn't be a problem. The weather had been mild the last few days, but she knew it would be colder in Bowness Park than downtown.

"I'll be there as soon as I can," Margie promised.

As Margie stood up and got ready to go, Detective Katelyn Jones was returning to her desk after getting coffee from the breakroom

"Parks Pat is on call," Margie advised Jones. "Bowness Park."

"Have fun," Jones told her cheerfully. "Don't worry about the rest of us, stuck at our desks flipping through dusty cold cases."

"Well, I guess I've got a cold case of my own," Margie laughed.

CHAPTER TWO

*M*argie worried at first that she had taken a wrong turn, it was taking so long to drive to Bowness Park. She didn't remember it being so far west. She had thought it just the other side of Crowchild Trail, but it was a long way past that. The GPS wasn't objecting that she had missed a turn, so she kept going, following the instructions as they were dictated to her and shown on the screen.

Then she did miss the turn into the park. The entrance was well-hidden. Margie swore when the GPS instructed her to perform a U-turn to get back to the park.

After she got turned around and took another run at it, she found the initial descent into the park familiar even after all the years since she had been there as a child. Margie knew she was in the right place.

She spotted a police car in the main parking lot and an officer stood nearby with a black mask, high-vis traffic vest, and orange baton, chatting with park patrons. It was evident that there wasn't much for him to do there. All of the experts were probably there ahead of Margie.

She drove up slowly, waiting for him to finish talking with an older couple before turning his attention to her.

"Detective Patenaude," Margie announced herself after rolling down the window and letting the brisk air in.

"Ah, Detective. You are this way," he pointed the baton to the roadway she should take. "Just keep following it around. You won't be able to miss all of the other vehicles."

"Thank you."

She rolled the window up again. Gagnon was obviously right about her needing to dress warmly. It was always colder near the water and there was a brisk wind.

She followed the road around and, after a couple of kilometers, found the site of the accident.

She had a lot more winter gear in her trunk than she needed walking only from her house to the car and the car to the office. But she always preached preparedness to Christina. A person couldn't trust that the car would always work and that she wouldn't have a breakdown or get into a motor vehicle accident and end up standing at the side of the road or pushing the car out of an intersection. Margie pulled on ski pants, swapped her shoes for boots, put a puffy vest on under her coat, and bundled up with her warmest gloves, hat, and face covering.

She felt like the Michelin Man as she walked to the line of vehicles and the people gathered there ahead of her. She found Gagnon with a couple of patrolmen with red noses and Tim's coffee cups.

He was a heavy man, made to look even rounder with the bulk of his winter jacket. His face mask was pulled down to drink the coffee, and there was frost in his mustache.

He nodded a greeting to her. "I'm sure everyone knows Parks Pat," he said, without bothering to introduce any of the other law enforcement officers to her. "Found it okay?"

"Yeah, no problem." Or only one, anyway. Margie gazed

out at the river. While there was ice and snow at the edges, there was still a wide channel of dark water running down the center. Too early in the season for it to be completely iced over. Even when it was, people would need to be careful and know how thick or thin the ice was. She had seen cars drive on the river when it was fully iced in, but she wouldn't choose to walk on it herself. She would stick to the pond, lagoon, or irrigation ditches. Nothing with fast-moving water. She knew enough about the river to respect it.

There were a number of figures out on the ice dressed in dark coats, too far away for her to make out the insignia. A yellow raft had been inflated but sat unused on the ice. Some men in wet suits stood around talking as if they didn't have a care in the world and were completely unaffected by the cold.

"So, what have we got?" she asked.

"Body discovered in the river," Gagnon pointed to a bright fleck of color at the edge of the ice. "Got caught on a log. They're going to attempt to retrieve the body in a few minutes."

"Did anyone see it happen? Do we know who it is?"

"No. Someone walking over the bridge saw it," Gagnon shifted his pointing finger to the wide bridge past the body caught on the log. "They called it in and, gradually, we got everyone out here to discuss the best way to retrieve it. The ice is thick enough over here," he pointed to the larger group of people, "but not out there," he indicated the men in the wet suits. "They are trained in cold water rescue, so this is their thing. I don't know yet whether they will go out in the boat and approach it from the water or see if they can crawl out on the ice and pull it in that way."

Margie shuddered. "Better them than me. I don't think I'll be volunteering to be part of *that* team."

"Wouldn't get me out there either," Gagnon agreed. "I had a friend drown when I was a teenager. Playing on the ice before it was safe." He shook his head. "Ice opened up right in front of me. Water was as black as pitch. Like a gateway to hell."

Margie shuddered, even though she was warm in her winter clothing, at the thought of seeing something like that happen right before her eyes. Or worse, having it happen to her. She could imagine the ice water closing in around her, chilling her to the bone and pulling her under.

"That's horrible," she told Gagnon.

He made one of those indescribably French grunts of acknowledgment. "Oui."

Margie smiled. "We say *oui* too, but we spell it w-i-i."

He raised his brows inquiringly. "What?"

"In Michif. The Métis language. We say *wii*."

"Ah." He nodded. "It is all a bastardized French, is it not? Pidgin?"

Margie resisted the urge to snap at him. He knew something about Michif at least, and was making an inquiry to understand more. It was good to ask questions, even if she didn't like his approach.

"From my understanding of the definitions, it is a creole, not a pidgin."

"Creole like New Orleans?" He shook his head. "It's not the same."

"A creole is two different languages joining to become a new language. A pidgin is a simplified version of a language. Some say Michif is creole and some say it isn't. But it is a mix of French and Cree and some other influences."

Gagnon nodded. "I see."

The men out on the ice began to move. Margie watched the men in wet suits begin to push the raft. But they didn't push it out into the river as she had expected them to. They pushed it along the ice toward the point where the body was caught on a branch or log. Margie and Gagnon watched, both tense.

As the men in wet suits got closer to the body, Margie

heard the ice cracking. She looked down at her feet as if cracks might appear there, but she was standing on the shore and didn't need to worry that the cracks in the ice would extend to her feet. Then she looked at the other law enforcement officers and techs standing halfway out. What if the cracks in the ice extended to them?

But they watched, seeming unconcerned. Maybe someone had measured the thickness of the ice and had already established that it was safe at that point. There were a lot of them standing too close together for Margie's comfort, putting a lot of weight on that one part of the ice. She could just picture the shelf breaking off and floating down the river with them still on it.

There were louder pops and cracks of ice under the raft, sounding like gunshots in the distance. There were shouts from the men in wet suits, and then, all at once, the ice beneath the raft broke, and they all slipped into the raft, as graceful as swans, as if that was what they had planned to do all along. Maybe it was.

They controlled the movement of the raft with paddles and poles and snugged it up against the log so that a couple of them could work on freeing the body while the other held the craft in place. Margie was breathing through her open mouth, panting as hard as if she were the one doing all the physical work.

If they went into the water, they would be fine. They were dressed for it. They had trained for it. But she could barely breathe, waiting for them to fall in. Gagnon too was tense, looking like he would grab her if things did not go well. They made a good pair.

Margie blew out a shaky breath and tried to laugh at herself, but the high giggle that came out of her would not fool anyone.

With a great heave, the rescuers managed to pull the body

into the raft. They then pushed it away from the log and continued to travel downstream. A few meters farther down, there was a clean shelf of ice. They got close to it, and then two of them jumped out, grabbed the ropes along the side of the raft, and pulled it up onto the ice.

They pulled the raft to the shore, laughing and shouting as if they were having the time of their lives. Margie supposed they were high on adrenaline after tempting fate in the icy water.

Once the raft was pulled to the shore, everyone moved toward it, picking their way through the brush and rocks to reach it and look inside.

"There's your ice queen," one of the men in a wet suit announced. "None the worse for wear."

"Nicely done," said one of the law enforcement officers who had been watching the operation from the safety of the ice. "What about other forensics? Trace on the log? Any other foreign materials caught in the branches?"

"Nothing obvious. Just her and some twigs. Flotsam."

Margie was close enough to see that the man who approached the body first was a crime scene tech she had run into at other sites. She stayed back and waited for him to take pictures and examine the woman's outer clothing.

The victim had obviously not intended to go for a swim. She wasn't prepared for the possibility like the men in the wet suits. The heavy clothing she wore would have pulled her down immediately, dragging her under the water. The icy water would quickly have incapacitated her and made it impossible for her to get herself back to safety. Margie's throat closed as she thought of being dragged under the surface by the weight of her clothes.

The tech muttered to his companions as they examined the body carefully, documenting everything.

"Was her coat torn before you pulled her off of the branch?"

The foremost man in a wet suit shrugged. "It was after we pulled her off."

The tech shook his head in irritation.

Margie thought that the men had done well, considering the circumstances. No one had been hurt or ended up in the water, and they were able to retrieve the body on the first try and not dump her back in the water. All in all, it was a pretty successful venture and not one that she would have volunteered for.

The tech eventually unbuttoned the heavy winter coat to give them a better look at the body.

It was a woman, as the rescuer had indicated. She had long hair frozen into intertwining sticks in a mass around her head. She had a couple of scrapes and bruises on her pale white face. The body under the coat was not slim. Not all of the bulk was the coat—a lot of it was the woman herself. The rescuers must have both been pretty strong to be able to move a woman of her size, especially a dead weight, clothing soaked in water.

The tech described the woman into a hand-held digital recorder, estimating her height and weight.

"She doesn't look like she's been dead long," Margie said. She had seen bodies bloated up in the water, features unrecognizable. Maybe it took longer when the water was so cold.

"No, don't think so," the tech told her after turning off his recorder. "Last night, probably. And she wasn't completely submerged, snagged on the log like that."

Margie nodded. She didn't take out her notebook to note down this information. She would save as much writing as she could for when she was back in her car with the heater on and the doors shut to keep out the wind. Her gloved fingers tingled from the cold despite the layers of insulation she had bundled herself in.

"Any identification?" Gagnon asked.

The tech patted her coat and shook his head. "Will have to check more carefully at the morgue. No obvious wallet. But most women carry their wallet in a purse, not coat pockets."

"No purse?" Margie asked. "Nothing caught on the log?"

"No. Might want to conduct a search downriver, see if it washed up on shore."

CHAPTER THREE

*T*here wasn't much to be discovered at the scene. The techs scouted both upstream and downstream, hoping to identify the spot where the woman had gone into the water or whether any of her possessions had washed up, but the snow and ice obscured any evidence of the accident scene. There were numerous animal tracks along the way where birds had landed or other animals had walked out to drink from the river. Quite a few human tracks, too. Margie was surprised by the number of people who had walked out onto the ice without any apparent concern for their safety. It was impossible to tell when the victim had crossed the ice or where she had entered the water.

"Accident?" Margie proposed to Gagnon as they stripped off their winter gear at the office. The indoor air seemed almost too warm after her time in the frigid outside weather.

"We'll see what the Office of the Chief Medical Examiner has to say," Gagnon said with a shrug of his bulky shoulders. "OCME gets the final say."

"But that's what it looked like to you?"

"Not a shooting or a stabbing, no apparent injuries other

than a smack or two on the head. She could have been drunk or drugged. A lot of people who die of hypothermia are."

Margie hadn't smelled any alcohol, but she wasn't sure that she had been close enough to. "She seemed well put together. Good clothes, manicured nails."

Gagnon nodded. "Doesn't rule out being drunk."

"No, of course not," Margie agreed. Plenty of rich people got drunk occasionally or were closet alcoholics. The same held for drug use. And since the legalization of marijuana, there were a lot more people experimenting or indulging on special occasions. People in all walks of life, some taking it for recreation and some for chronic pain or nausea.

"What was someone like her even doing at the park at night, though?" Gagnon asked.

"We haven't established for sure that it was at night."

"No, but you would think that if she had gone in the water during the day, someone would have noticed and called for help. Or would have told her to stay off of the ice or away from the edge."

"True," Margie conceded. She couldn't see how either scenario worked. She couldn't see a reason for the woman to go to the edge of the ice on the river during the day or the night. Maybe she lived in one of the houses near the park and had sleepwalked into the water. It had been known to happen. The cold water would have woken her up but, once she was in the water, it was too late. Margie just couldn't see any other way it might have happened. Unless... "Suicide?" she suggested. "Maybe it was intentional."

"What a way to go," Gagnon said, shaking his head. His dark eyes were haunted. Remembering the friend he had lost? The ice opening up like the gates of hell in front of him? She wondered how the experience had affected him over the years.

"Not the way I would choose," Margie agreed. "But it

would be quick. And no way to change your mind once you were in."

∮

CHRISTINA CALLED to check in with Margie when she got home from school. "We're getting close to the Indigenous Fair," Christina commented before either of them had a chance to talk about how their days had gone. "I can't believe it. When it was rescheduled, I thought we had plenty of time to get everything done, and now... there's no time left!"

"Not much," Margie agreed with a smile. "You'll be glad to have it off your plate when it's done."

"Will I ever. I feel like I haven't done anything else this year, just organizing the darn thing. It was a lot more work than I thought it would be. I pictured... putting a few posters up and people volunteering to do booths or presentations, and that's it. It would all just come together by itself. But it's been such a lot of work."

And soon, she would need to study for her first semester final exams. Margie hoped Christina would use some of the Christmas break to do practice tests and prepare for finals. Everyone was anxious about whether the kids had learned everything they were supposed to during the COVID lockdown and then so many students and teachers being out sick during the Delta wave.

They had been through a lot.

"So, how are you, Mom?" Christina asked, probably having heard Margie's sigh over the phone line.

"Caught a new case today. Bowness Park."

"Parks Pat is at it again," Christina said lightly. "What happened?"

"Drowning. In the river, last night probably."

"Oh, great case for you," Christina sympathized, knowing of Margie's phobia of water.

"Well, luckily, I didn't have to get too close. There was a water rescue team to get her out, so I just stayed on the shore and watched. But it was still… whew… It still affected me."

"Of course," Christina agreed. "That's scary. Do you know who she was? How did she get in the water? Did she fall out of a boat?"

That was one scenario that Margie hadn't considered.

"No, I don't think so. It's not completely iced over—there is a channel down the center where a boat could go—but I don't think many people would do that this time of year; I don't think it would be safe. And a lot of people would notice. We think… well, we're still figuring out what we think, but we think she fell through the ice. It's too thin for people to walk on yet, and maybe she didn't know that."

She could practically hear Christina rolling her eyes. "If there is a channel down the center, you'd be pretty stupid to think it was thick enough to walk on."

"Yes. But we don't know. It could have been night and she couldn't see across. She could have been sleepwalking. It could have been suicide. Or just… I don't know; sometimes people don't think about what they are doing. 'I walked on the ice yesterday and it was fine, so I can walk on it more today…'"

"People are stupid sometimes," Christina admitted with a sigh. "So, does that mean you won't be home for dinner?"

"I think I should still be home for dinner. Let's plan on it, and I'll try to give you a heads-up if things change."

"Yeah." Christina didn't sound like she believed Margie. "Just let me know if you're running late."

"I will."

CHAPTER FOUR

"OCME has posted preliminary results," Gagnon announced from across the bullpen.

Margie frowned as she looked across the room at him. "Really? That's quick."

"I don't think it was that complicated a case. Maybe there were no other autopsies waiting and they were able to jump right into it."

Margie opened the workspace on her computer screen, and the first thing she noticed was the name.

"And she was identified?"

"She must have had ID on her after all."

Gagnon walked over and looked at it with her. He apparently preferred looking over Margie's shoulder at the result.

"Julia Louise Robertson," Margie read, "Do I know that name from somewhere?"

Jones gave a little gasp and turned toward Margie with wide eyes. "Julia Louise Robertson? She's an investigative reporter."

The gears in Margie's brain were turning. How did an investigative journalist end up drowning one night in Bowness

Park? Everything suddenly took on a new light. Somebody who was just stupid and happened to be walking on the ice where it was too thin? She recalled the woman's elegant attire and perfectly manicured nails. No. It hadn't just been a casual walk, going out farther onto the ice than was advisable. She was too smart for that. And too wealthy for that neighborhood. She was a celebrated journalist, the kind who had won multiple awards and rubbed elbows with the country's rich and famous. She would not be living in Bowness. Margie had seen a few really nice houses there where people had built mini mansions for themselves, but the ones in the immediate neighborhood to the park were much more modest, and Margie couldn't see someone like Julia Louise Robertson living there.

"Do you think that's why they pushed the autopsy through so quickly?" Jones asked. "They figured out who it was and decided to prioritize it?"

Margie nodded. "It's possible. They probably want to have a preliminary answer before people start calling in demanding answers. This is one where the mayor will be calling, maybe even the prime minister. You don't want to put those guys off too long." She breathed out. "Julia Louise Robertson!"

"You're not going to find anything else out saying her name," Gagnon said irritably. "Click on the preliminary report by the ME."

Margie obeyed. There was no point in swooning over the identity of the victim. Where was that going to get her? She clicked on the report and skimmed it.

"Consistent with drowning. Water in the lungs. Likely incapacitated by the cold when she fell into the water. Scrapes and bruises on her head and face, both antemortem and postmortem."

"Got banged up in the river," Jones contributed.

"Running into a log will do that," Gagnon agreed.

"No defensive marks on hands. No other marks on the body. All consistent with accidental drowning."

"Tox results," Gagnon ordered. "I want to see the tox results."

Margie scrolled down. "Preliminary tox results. Field tests only. Negative for alcohol and the most popular recreational drugs."

"Negative." Gagnon was breathing on Margie's neck. His voice was tight as if he were angry. "I was sure the woman had been drinking. Why else would she end up in the river?"

Margie scratched the back of her neck and put her hand over it to keep Gagnon's breathing from raising goosebumps on her skin.

"So are they finding that it was an accident?" Jones asked. "I don't hear anything that rules out homicide or suicide."

"It wasn't homicide," Gagnon disagreed. "There is nothing to indicate any violence. She was out there by herself."

Jones looked at Margie, brows raised, to see what she thought. Margie shook her head. "I don't know. No preliminary manner of death. Just that the cause was cold water drowning."

"No point in looking for something that's not there," Gagnon said flatly.

"No," Margie agreed. "But this is not the final report. And we haven't completed our investigation."

"What's to investigate?" Gagnon challenged. "I'm ready to close it."

"Well, now that we know who it is, maybe interview her family and friends, see what her state of mind was lately. What she was working on. If anything unusual was going on in her life. If she regularly walked along the river."

Gagnon grunted. "I suppose we're going to have to go through the motions. Since she's someone famous. They'll accuse us of being part of a conspiracy if we don't."

"Yeah," Margie agreed. "Exactly. We don't need that kind of publicity."

Jones chuckled.

Margie clicked through the other files on the workspace—pictures of the autopsy, the clothing, jewelry, and pocket contents. Margie's own notes and Gagnon's were there as well, but she already knew what was in them.

She scrolled through the pocket contents and found that they included a reporter's notebook. Not just a cheap loonie store notebook, but a good quality one that hadn't dissolved when it got wet. The ME had carefully pressed and photographed each page while they dried. Most of it was in the reporter's shorthand. She abbreviated words and used initials to signify the people she was interviewing. She quickly jotted phrases about things that she wanted to be able to remember, but that didn't mean anything to anyone else. Margie scrolled to the end to see what the last thing was that Julia Louise Robertson had written.

CHAPTER FIVE

ENCOUNTER WITH THE ICEBERG

*M*argie stared at the words, trying to decipher their meaning. She was, of course, misreading something. Robertson hadn't been concerned about an iceberg. She wasn't on the Titanic. Maybe it was the title of a piece she was planning to write. Something about a problem that was mainly beneath the surface. Menacing. Margie hoped to uncover its meaning when she reviewed the remaining notes in the reporter's notepad.

"What is it?" Jones asked, unable to see Margie's screen from where she was sitting.

Gagnon leaned closer to the screen to squint at the words as if they were too small and he couldn't make sense of them.

"Encounter with the iceberg," he read to Jones.

"What the heck is that supposed to mean?"

"I don't know," Margie said. "Probably the title of an article she was writing."

"Oh, that would make sense, yeah."

Gagnon withdrew again so his face wasn't right beside

Margie's. "Who knows what a reporter is thinking," he said as if reporters were a mysterious species of their own.

"It's just weird," Jones said. "That she would write about an iceberg and then fall through the ice and drown…"

They all considered this.

"Yeah," Margie admitted. "It is weird."

"Do you think it was a premonition? Maybe she'd had a dream about it?"

Margie looked at her. She had never known Jones to be superstitious before.

"I don't know what it's about, but I'm sure it will make sense once we've had a chance to read the rest of her materials. Maybe we can request the files she was working on from the network."

"Good luck with that," Gagnon said. "They'll never give up her files, even with a subpoena. You know how reporters are."

"But if something about it got her killed…"

"There's no indication that this is a homicide, so how are you going to persuade a judge of that? We're lucky to have the notebook that was in her pocket. Maybe there will be something interesting in there. Hopefully, something a little more enlightening than 'beware the iceberg.'"

"It didn't say 'beware the iceberg.' It says, 'encounter with the iceberg.'" Margie corrected, clicking back on the note to ensure she got it right.

"Whatever. If you're going to encounter an iceberg, you'd better beware." Gagnon snorted at his own cleverness.

Margie and Jones shook their heads. Margie looked at the time on her phone. "Well, I'd better be getting out of here. Kiddo is expecting me."

"Have a good night," Jones chirped. "Say 'hi' to Christina for me. I'll see you tomorrow."

Margie nodded. She started to get ready to go, closing the workspace and her other apps, locking her screen, and getting her purse out of the desk drawer. Gagnon was still standing behind her. She looked at him.

"Was there something else?"

"You'll do interviews with me tomorrow?" he asked.

"Yeah. Of course. You can call and set up whatever you can tonight. I'll be here in the morning, and we can go after the stand-up meeting."

He nodded his agreement. "*Oui.* Tomorrow then. *Bon.*"

"*Boon,*" Margie agreed with a smile.

CHAPTER SIX

*M*argie checked the clock on the dashboard as she arrived at the house to ensure she was not too late. She had left the office downtown in good time, but there had been a couple of traffic snarls on the way home, so she ended up being later than she had expected.

The front light was turned on. Margie let herself in. Stella leaped off the bed in Christina's room with a thump, and her paws drummed against the floor as she raced across the house. As soon as she reached the door, she started barking excitedly and jumping around Margie.

"Hi, Stella," Margie stopped to give her pets and scratch her ears. "Who's a good girl? Were you a good girl while I was at work today? Of course you were a good girl. You're always a good girl, aren't you?"

Stella settled down so that she was sitting quietly in front of Margie, her tail beating the floor.

Christina was a bit slower getting to the living room to greet Margie.

"Hey." She looked a little sleepy, and Margie wondered whether she'd been having a nap before Margie had arrived home. "I didn't start on dinner yet because I didn't know what time you were *actually* going to get home. Sometimes when you have a new case…"

"I know. Things can get crazy. But I'm not the lead on this one, and I said I needed to get home. We'll be doing interviews tomorrow. There isn't much I could do tonight anyway."

"Well, good," Christina approved. "Do you want to make something or go out for food?"

They almost always made their own food, and Christina rarely asked to go out for fast food, so it was an unusual question.

"Did you want to go out somewhere?" Margie asked, pausing in unbuttoning her coat.

"Well, we could. If you're too tired to make dinner."

"I could make dinner. But you sound like you wanted to go somewhere."

"I just think it's been a long time since we went for pizza or anything."

"You're right, it has been. Do you want to go out? Get a nice veggie pizza?"

Christina nodded. "Yeah. It would be nice to get something tonight."

"Delivery?" Margie asked.

"No, we should pick something up. So much cheaper."

The family finances were not usually Christina's concern either, though Margie tried to involve her in decision-making. It was just the two of them, and Margie wanted Christina to have some say in how their finances were handled. What things they saved money on and where they splurged. She wanted Christina to understand how finances worked when she moved out on her own.

"Okay," Margie agreed. "We'll go for pizza, then."

She had to wonder if there were something more behind Christina's suggestion to go out for pizza. Like she was going to bring up a topic that she would rather bring up with other people around so that Margie couldn't yell at her.

She remembered using that strategy on her own mother. It had, unfortunately, not worked out as well as she had hoped. She had still been in trouble. She had been embarrassed in front of friends and strangers instead of just in front of her family members at home.

"Everything going okay at school?" she asked tentatively once they were in the car, driving slowly down Seventeenth Avenue to pick out a pizzeria.

"Yeah, just like I said. Trying to get everything to work out for the Indigenous Fair. I'm afraid people are tired of hearing it now and will just want to drop it. But some of the kids still seem excited about it."

"That's good. Don't worry about the rest. Even if you only educate one person, you never know how far that can spread and how much good it can do."

"Well, I hope I educate more than one person."

"I know."

More silence.

"And you're going to get some studying done over Christmas break?" Margie suggested. "So that you'll be ready for finals?"

"I really don't want to write finals," Christina groaned.

"Nobody does. It's just one of those things we have to put up with."

"I'll study," Christina said tiredly. "Let me get through the Indigenous Fair and Christmas first."

She sounded worn out. Margie resolved to keep a better eye on her mood and whether she was getting enough sleep.

"Don't look at me like that," Christina growled. "There's nothing wrong with me."

"No, I'm just concerned. You'll tell me if you're feeling burned out or depressed, won't you? We can do things to manage it. But I don't want you trying to handle things alone. People who try to manage all of their emotional issues by themselves end up getting in trouble."

"I'm not depressed. I'm just tired."

Margie looked away from the road to study Christina for a long moment at a red light.

"Okay," she agreed. "Just let me know. I'm here any time you need to talk."

CHAPTER SEVEN

*A*s soon as Margie walked in the office door, she was accosted by Detective Gagnon. He wore a scowl, black brows drawn down.

"We have a lot of work to get done today," he told her as if she were late getting in. "Interviews are lined up, and the bigwigs are already manning the phones, asking why it is taking us so long to get traction on the case."

"Robertson was only identified yesterday," Margie pointed out in consternation, "and the ME has only released preliminary findings. Exactly what were we supposed to have done already that we haven't?"

"Press and politicians are not well-known for their logic," Gagnon said sourly. "But they *are* known for being impatient and making a lot of noise. So we need to get to work."

Margie motioned toward the briefing room. "We still need to do morning briefing. We can't exactly get started before that is done."

"I've briefed MacDonald privately. We need to hit the pavement."

"No stand-up meeting?"

"Not for you and me. MacDonald will fill everyone else in; we're to get started."

"Well, okay." Margie had been unbuttoning her coat, but she stopped. If they were going back out again right away, there was no point in taking it off. "Just give me a minute to grab a coffee, and then we can head out."

Gagnon nodded impatiently. But Margie was already dressed and ready to go, and he was not. She was sure it would take her no longer to get her coffee than for him to get his coat and other winter gear on.

He was faster than she expected and was waiting at the door, looking at his watch when she stepped out of the breakroom.

"All right, ready to go?" Margie asked him, as if she had been waiting for him to get ready. Otherwise, he would make more impatient noises at her for having to stop to get coffee. But she needed the boost to get her brain going, especially if they were interviewing right away, without a chance to warm up and bounce ideas off of the other detectives and make sure that they had all of their bases covered.

Gagnon led the way to his car. He looked sourly at Margie's travel mug as she settled it into one of the cup holders. But she hadn't spilled a drop on the pristine surfaces of his car. Which were actually not all that pristine. She hadn't noticed the smell of cigarette smoke clinging to Gagnon before, but either he or someone else smoked in the car, and several cups and food wrappers hadn't been cleared out of the car. So what objection could he have to her drinking coffee in the car?

"Who are we seeing today?" she asked briskly.

"First off is John Calver, ex-husband,"

Exes were always a good bet when looking into an unexpected death. If it turned out that there had been foul play, the spouse or ex-spouse was always the first suspect.

"What do we know about him?"

"They married before she became well-established as an investigative journalist. So he's not... high society. They were fairly young, fresh out of school, idealistic, you know how kids are."

Margie nodded, thinking of her daughter. How long would she stay passionate and idealistic? She was eager to educate others on her Indigenous heritage and culture and that of the other Indigenous nations in the area. How long would it be before she became discouraged by those uninterested in what she had to tell them? Or would she become an advocate for her people long-term, joining up with the Native Friendship Center or one of the other organizations dedicated to education?

She sipped her coffee and focused on the job at hand. John Calver.

"How long were they together?"

"Twenty years or so. Whether they were together that whole time or not, I'm not sure. Looks like it was a somewhat rocky relationship. He did acquire more than one domestic violence charge."

"Oh, did he?"

Gagnon nodded.

"Well, that's interesting. What was the breakup like? Acrimonious?"

He glanced sideways at her. "Acrimonious?"

"Were they on good terms? Or was there a lot of conflict between them? Bitter feelings?"

"I know what acrimony is."

Then why had he challenged her use of the word? Margie gave a slight head shake.

"I wasn't able to find out too much about it yesterday," Gagnon admitted. "We'll have to see what we can find out from talking to him. We can do a courthouse search on the divorce file to see what documents were filed and what allegations were made if we need to. See what feeling we get from this guy."

Margie nodded. "Okay."

At least they weren't going into it blind. They knew that there had been domestic violence.

"You ever married?" Gagnon asked.

"Me? No. You?"

He snorted. "*Non.*"

There seemed to be a lot hidden beneath his answer, but Margie didn't think she had the time or energy to explore it. Gagnon's personal life was his own. She didn't need to know his history. They needed to find out what had happened in Julia's life.

CHAPTER EIGHT

*J*ohn Calver was also a journalist, though from the small, dirty storefront his paper operated out of, it was a rag. He had not achieved anything near the distinction Robertson had. Margie had never heard of the paper, but that didn't mean it lacked readership. She was only aware of the main city papers and news magazines on TV. Alternative press wasn't something she had any experience in.

Calver himself was a pugnacious-looking, olive-skinned man. No longer a young man, he was going gray at his sideburns and had dark rings under his eyes. The normal state of affairs, or had he been up all night thinking about his dead ex-wife?

"Mr. Calver, good to meet you," Margie greeted pleasantly. She didn't offer her hand and, in keeping with the times, neither did he or Gagnon. Calver wasn't wearing a mask, but didn't object to Margie and Gagnon wearing theirs, which suited Margie just fine. That allowed them to see his expressions more clearly, but to better keep their own thoughts more private.

"Our condolences on the passing of your ex-wife," Gagnon offered.

Calver pointed to a flimsy-looking table in the middle of the floor surrounded by mismatched chairs that might have been scrounged from a back alley.

"Things were over with Julia and me a long time ago."

Margie wasn't sure it was true. He looked pretty rough for someone who had not been personally affected by Julia Louise Robertson's death. But maybe his apparent dissolution was the normal state of affairs.

"How did things end between the two of you?" Margie asked once they were seated.

"We both agreed that it was time to end things. We didn't get along so well together. We had gone in separate directions over the years. Didn't really have anything in common anymore."

"It happens," Gagnon said understandingly.

Calver looked toward him and seemed to connect with him better than with Margie. "People don't expect to stay together forever these days. Even though you're showing your commitment through marriage, you know it isn't likely to last more than a few years."

"Twenty years is a good run."

"Yeah, that's what I thought. We gave it our best shot but, eventually… well, things happen. She had her career, which didn't leave much time for anything else. Our politics were different. We didn't share the same friends. We didn't share much, to be honest."

"So it made sense to formalize the separation."

"Yeah. Neither one of us really wanted the divorce, but we didn't want to stay together, either."

"Might as well be legally free of each other," Gagnon agreed. "Split the assets. Be able to see other people without complications. Go your separate directions."

"Yeah."

"Did the two of you stay in touch?" Margie asked.

"I kept track of what she was doing. And we did have a few friends in common that would mention her now and then. But direct contact… no. There was no need. Neither of us had any desire."

"So it was a pretty clean break."

He nodded. "Yes. I think it's nonsense, the whole business of 'staying friends' and still getting together for coffee or seeing each other socially after the divorce. I didn't want to have any more contact with her. That was the whole point of the divorce."

"Sure."

"I was shocked to hear about what had happened to her, very sorry to have her go that way. But there isn't anything I can help you with. I wasn't a part of her life anymore. What she would have been doing in Bowness Park or on the river—" he shook his head, "I have no idea. That wasn't her kind of thing. Very out of character."

"She didn't go for walks?"

"No. If you've seen pictures of her, you know she wasn't exactly a lightweight. She wasn't interested in exercise. Not walking or going to the gym. She drove everywhere or had a service take her. She wasn't into parks and nature."

"What was she into?"

"It was all about her work. She was into whatever she was investigating at the moment. She worked, ate, and slept what-ever story she was investigating. It was all about revealing the truth."

"And you don't know what she was working on recently? What story she might have been running down?"

"No, sorry. No idea."

"Did she ever say anything to you about an iceberg?"

He shook his head, brows drawing down. "Do you mean, like, an actual iceberg?"

"We don't know. That's what we're trying to figure out."

"We didn't talk. I don't know when the last time was that I had a conversation with her. Nothing about an iceberg."

Margie nodded understandingly. She looked at Gagnon, who took up the next line of questioning.

"What were things like when the two of you were together? I notice that there were a few domestic violence charges."

"I was never convicted," Calver said immediately. "Nothing ever stuck. The cops, they're told that they have to lay domestic violence charges whenever there is a disturbance call and a couple is arguing about something. It doesn't mean there was any actual violence."

"The two of you only argued?" Gagnon asked.

"We were a married couple with separate interests. Of course we argued. That's pretty much the only kind of conversation we had in the final months. It doesn't mean that I was beating her."

"You never laid hands on her?"

"I was never convicted of anything. What does that tell you?"

It didn't tell Margie that he *wasn't* guilty of intimate partner violence. It just meant there had not been enough proof to do anything about it. Maybe Julia had refused to testify against him, so the prosecutor hadn't had anything but the report of the police officers who had responded that she'd had a fresh bruise on her face. And that wasn't proof of anything but that she'd hit her face on something recently. She could have walked into a door like she told them. Or hit herself. Or been in a fight with a neighbor. Or the subject in a story she had been investigating.

It was almost impossible to get a conviction against a husband when his victim was shielding him.

"How many assaults?" Gagnon asked.

"What?"

"How many times were you charged? I can look it up."

Calver hesitated. He could tell Gagnon to go ahead, look it up, to be belligerent and refuse to answer. But he was trying to give the impression that he felt bad about Julia and was being helpful and cooperative. And maybe he didn't want them digging into his history and could avoid it by answering the question.

"Four times," he answered finally. His tone was flat. It was just a fact. Not something that he had to defend himself about. Not something to get excited about. It didn't mean he was a bad person. He and his wife had grown apart and had neighbors who felt it necessary to intervene when they argued.

But four was over the edge, in Margie's opinion. It was easy for a man to have the police come down on him once when he was completely innocent. Maybe his wife *had* scratched herself. Maybe he'd been drunk and taken a swing at her in front of the police, even though he had never connected and never intended to. Maybe she had simply made accusations when he had never laid a hand on her, and the police had done their duty in taking the statement.

But after that, he would be more careful. Maybe he'd get another accusation from another girlfriend ten years later when they were in the midst of a breakup.

But being charged four times for violence against his wife, that was a lot. And only the tip of the iceberg, if Margie were to borrow a term from Julia. There was no chance he had been charged every time he had been violent toward his wife. Or even half the time. They should probably check emergency room visits and see how often Julia had been treated for injuries that might have been the result of a domestic assault.

"Where were you the night before last?" Gagnon asked in the same flat tone as Calver had used.

Calver looked like he would object, would raise a fuss to point out how stupid they were being, since he didn't have anything to do with Julia anymore and had been nowhere near Bowness Park. But he schooled himself, pressing his lips together and maybe counting to ten before responding. His chin lifted a little.

"Having a drink with some friends."

"Mind if I get their names and phone numbers to confirm that?"

"That's an invasion of privacy," Calver objected. "You can't go around bugging my friends…"

"We will be discreet. But we would be remiss not to check your alibi."

Calver made more noises of objection, mostly to himself, but he pulled out his phone and gave Gagnon several names and phone numbers. The fact that he had them at hand was a good sign. They would call as soon as they separated from Calver to ensure he didn't have a chance to call them and encourage them to give a false story. If the alibi checked out, they could take Calver off of their list of suspects. Chances were that he hadn't hired or encouraged someone else to kill her so long after the divorce was over and done. People who wanted their wives killed did it while they were still married.

CHAPTER NINE

*W*here next?" Margie asked.

"Her workplace. The network."

"Oh, that's going to be fun."

They would be juggling competing interests. The network wanted Julia's death to be investigated by the police and the culprit brought to justice. Still, they would also be asserting their right to keep sources confidential and to keep any information they had that might relate to Julia's death to themselves so that they could have an exclusive exposé on her story.

And television networks were not the calmest, most sane places to work or conduct an interview to begin with.

"Do we have the name of someone to talk to?" Margie asked.

"We've been getting all kinds of phone calls. I have a few names."

Margie snorted and shook her head. Of course. The network had not sat quietly waiting for them to make the first move.

Outside the network's office, Margie and Gagnon stood for a few seconds, looking in at the bank of televisions inside the glass doors, showing what was currently playing, what was available for replay, and what was coming up. She wondered how much viewership they actually got from foot traffic walking by the building. Certainly enough to pay for a few extra monitors and feet of cable. The bright, flickering screens would suck in anyone who was walking by or waiting for the next bus or train.

Gagnon shrugged and pushed through the glass doors. They went in and found a reception desk. The woman manning it with a wireless headset was absurdly tall and thin, with short, spiked, bleached white hair and a sheath dress that belonged on a runway rather than at a receptionist's desk. Margie wondered how long the receptionist had been trying to break into network TV herself.

"We're here to see DeeDee Strong," Gagnon told her.

She waved him to silence for a moment, listening to something on her headset. She said okay a few times, then tapped to end the call.

"So sorry," she apologized. "DeeDee? Is she expecting you?"

"We're with the Calgary Police Service," Gagnon explained. "About Mrs. Robertson."

"Oh," the receptionist drew the syllable out long. "We are all in shock here. I can't believe… None of us could believe it when we heard. Like, I was sure it had to be some other Julia Louise Robertson… There are others. It's not that uncommon a name."

"I'm sure," Gagnon agreed. "It was very shocking. Now, if you could please direct us toward Mrs. Strong…"

"Are you talking to everyone who knew her?" the woman inquired. "That must be so fascinating. I'll bet you could write a book about her after that. Though you're not allowed to, you know…" She waggled her finger at them. "We have the exclusive rights to Julia's story."

"To her authorized biography, maybe," Gagnon said dryly. "That doesn't mean no one else can write about her."

The woman's mouth dropped open and she searched for something to say. Margie had to chuckle. "We wouldn't be allowed to write it as active police officers anyway," she told the woman. "I don't think you need to worry that we'll scoop you."

"Well, it's not *my* story," she muttered as she tapped numbers into the base of her phone. "Boy, if I was given *that* job…"

She interrupted herself as the call she had placed went through.

"DeeDee, honey, I'm sorry to bother you. I know you didn't want to be interrupted, but there are a couple of police officers here asking for you. They want to talk to you about Julia."

She listened attentively, hand up to prevent anyone from asking her anything. Then she nodded.

"Yes, of course, DeeDee. I'll look after everything."

She tapped to end the call and smiled at Gagnon and Margie.

"If you'll come with me, I'll get you set up in an interview room. DeeDee will join you just as soon as she is able."

They followed her into a well-appointed room, a small boardroom or large meeting room. Two walls were glass, with tiny Venetian blinds letting in light but still allowing a measure of privacy. The other walls held a stand for coffee service and a very large screen. The table and chairs were in a beautiful rose and silver theme, with a matching silk flower arrangement on the sideboard. The receptionist motioned for them to see down. "What can I get you to drink? Coffee? Tea? Cold drinks?"

"Just a water for me, please," Margie requested. She'd had her fill of coffee for the morning, but was finding herself dry after talking to Calver. Calgary's winter air was so dry, it seemed to suck the moisture out of everything.

Gagnon looked like he would refuse, then gave a little shrug with one shoulder. "Coffee," he requested.

"Certainly. DeeDee will be with you shortly."

She slid out of the room as smoothly and silently as if on rollers. Margie looked at Gagnon.

"Julia certainly climbed the ladder a little farther than her husband."

"Probably half the reason they divorced. Husbands don't like their wives being so much more successful than they are."

Margie would have liked to argue the point and say that was a biased viewpoint and certainly didn't apply to all couples. But it was true of most of the couples that she knew well. And from what she had seen of Calver, it was probably true of him. He was a journalist too. He didn't want to stand in his wife's shadow.

The receptionist returned with water and coffee and set them on the table. "Can I get you anything else?"

"No, thank you."

She looked hesitant about leaving but, eventually, she nodded and drifted away again like a ghost.

The next person to come into the room was not DeeDee, but a man in a vest and rolled-up sleeves, straight out of central casting. He stuck his head in the door and looked at Gagnon and Margie.

"Are you the detectives? Someone said that the detectives were here to talk to us."

"Well, yes…" Margie didn't want him to invite himself into the room when they were waiting for DeeDee. Yes, they were there to conduct interviews, but they wanted to keep everything under control. Not to spend their time with people who had nothing to do with Julia's death and didn't know anything about what cases she had been working on. "But…"

"Sebastian Doucet," he introduced himself, coming the rest of the way into the room. He put a foot up on the seat of the chair and leaned an elbow on his knee. Casual, or pretending to be casual. Not sitting down with them for an interview, but just happening to be there to exchange some gossip.

"Terrible, what happened to Julia," he said with relish.

"Yes, it is," Margie agreed. "I'm sure that you are devastated about it."

"Of course," he agreed, with no show of remorse whatsoever. "You must tell me everything you know about what happened to her. It is just unbelievable. It really is."

"We're not here to tell you about everything we have," Gagnon said in a measured tone. "We are here to make inquiries to find out what her coworkers might know about what she was working on."

"Oh, I doubt if anyone knew what she was working on. We are all very suspicious of each other and don't want to get scooped. So we don't share what we are working on until it is done and in the hopper."

Margie nodded slowly. "But her boss must have known what she was working on. The editor. Her cameraman. Whoever arranged for interviews for her."

"Julia did not get to be where she was by having loose lips. She played her cards close to the vest and made some very big stories. I'm sure you've read through the extremely long list of awards she had been given over the years. She was the cream of the crop. The network's pride and joy."

Gagnon looked Sebastian Doucet up and down. "Unlike you, who I don't remember hearing of before. What is it that you report on?"

"Oh, you've wounded me," Doucet said flamboyantly, with a hand to his breast. "I am following in Julia's footsteps! Maybe I'm not there yet, but I intend to be someday. I will be someday; you can count on that. No one is going to stop me."

A threat?

Had Julia been in his way? Someone that he perceived as blocking him from what he wanted to achieve? He certainly sounded like a jealous rival.

They both just looked at him, weighing his words. Margie got out her notebook and wrote his name in it. There. Now, he could revel in being a suspect. His name was in her notebook.

His eyes followed every movement, and he looked pleased —someone always glad to be in the spotlight.

CHAPTER TEN

a woman came to the door. Polished, chunky silver jewelry that coordinated and complemented the power suit she was wearing, navy, well-tailored to her shape. DeeDee Strong.

"What are you doing here?" she aimed the query at the man standing there with his foot on the chair. She looked as if she were searching her memory for his name. "Sebastian."

He cleared his throat and quickly removed his foot from the chair. "Ah, Miss Strong. Sorry, I was just… talking to the detectives. It's terrible what happened to Julia…"

"Yes, it is," the woman said. "And if you don't shove off, something could happen to you."

He made a movement halfway between a nod and a bow, and backed out of the room, nodding to each of the detectives. DeeDee watched him go and closed the door. She looked around the room as if to make sure it was secure. No one else there, no one watching, no recording devices or cameras. She let out a breath.

"I'm sure I wasn't that desperate and needy when I was a junior," she said, indicating the direction Sebastian had disappeared in. "But… it is a highly competitive business. People are always looking for a way to get one up on everyone else. To prove that they're the next big thing. It's just tooth and nail, pulling yourself up hand over hand to make something of yourself and get out there in front of an audience."

"So he's a junior?" Margie repeated. "He didn't actually know Julia?"

"Know her? Goodness, no. Not a chance. She wouldn't have had anything to do with him. The closest he might have gotten to her was to bring her a cup of coffee."

"And would she have thanked him for it?"

"Not likely," DeeDee sighed. "I'm sorry to portray the business in such a poor light, and maybe it's different at other networks, but we really can be…" She shook her head. "Selfish and self-centered, to put it politely."

"Won't you sit down?" Gagnon indicated the empty chairs at the table. "I got the names of several people at the network that want to talk to us or who might know something about Julia… But I picked you out as the person most likely to be able to help us. If you can't, hopefully you can point us in the right direction."

"I'll do my best."

"I got the feeling that you and Julia knew each other quite well. I'm not sure whether you were friends or rivals."

DeeDee spread her hands apart. "Both, I guess. We loved each other and were the best of friends. Loved to go out and do things together. But we were also always in competition. In everything. Breaking a story. Finding the perfect Christmas gift. It didn't matter what it was. We couldn't help ourselves."

"Is that because you were so much alike?" Margie suggested.

"Yes, I would say so. We were always after the same prize. Tended to think the same way. So it was pretty hard to stay out of each other's way. I don't know what I will do… now that she's gone. Things will be boring around here."

"You won't have anyone to compete with?"

"Well, there are still plenty of people to compete with, but it won't be the same. There aren't very many other people at my level. You might think I'm being egotistical, but it's the truth. People recognize our faces. We are household names. People know that if we bring them a story, it's going to be big. It's breaking news, and we will have uncovered something no one else could have. We're the best in the business."

Not egotistical at all.

"I wonder if you know anything that was going on in Julia's life. Anything unusual or concerning," Margie asked.

"Well, no, can't say I did. Everything seemed pretty normal. I mean, it was business as usual. She was working on an investigation. I was working on an investigation. As long as they don't intersect, you're golden. But if they collided with each other and we both ended up trying to chase the same lead, that was a problem."

"And did that happen? Do you know what she was working on?"

"No. I'm not sure what Julia was working on. It was something to do with Winnipeg." DeeDee mused on this for a minute. "Or, it was Manitoba, anyway. Maybe not Winnipeg. I don't remember—some kind of… financial scheme. I don't know. Maybe it was insider trading or something."

"In Winnipeg?" Gagnon questioned doubtfully, his French accent making him sound even more incredulous. What of any importance could come out of Winnipeg? Insider trading on what market?

"I didn't get the details," DeeDee said, brushing it aside. "Of course not. Neither of us would tell the other about anything we were investigating. No details."

"Did she say if she was dealing with anyone… dangerous? Did she have any concerns about it?"

DeeDee shook her head. She tapped the table with an acrylic nail as she thought about it. "I don't know. There was something. Something that she was excited about. But she didn't tell me what it was. She said that it was just the tip of the iceberg. Laughed about it."

Gagnon raised his brows at Margie. Another iceberg reference. But had Julia just been making a joke? Teasing her friend about the great new lead she had?

Margie opened the phone and thumbed over to the photo of the last page of Julia's notebook.

Encounter with the iceberg.

"What's that?" DeeDee asked. She squinted at it, frowning. "Is that Julia's notebook? Do you have it? I need to see that. We don't know what stories she might have been working on that we need to bring in. You need to get that to me. And her laptop, do you have that?"

"Somebody will be going by her house today," Gagnon told her. "We're just trying to find out who has access to her house. We can't just bust the door down like some TV show cops."

"I don't know who has access to her house. Maybe one of her neighbors. She didn't live with anyone."

"Did she date anyone after Calver?"

"Calver." DeeDee rolled her eyes. "Now there is a real winner. She dated, yes, but nothing long-term. No commitment."

"Was she afraid to after Calver, or did she just not have enough time?"

"It was all work with Julia. She didn't like to waste her time socializing. Me, I still like to have a little fun now and then. But Julia was married to the work. She would rather be working than anything else and didn't want anything to get in the way of that. Great work ethic. Horrible social life."

"If you have the names of anyone she was seeing lately…"

"No. I mean, you can check her phone. I don't have any names. It was all pretty casual. I doubt she went on more than one or two dates with anyone."

They would check her phone logs, and that should give them the names of anyone she had had social or professional contact with lately.

"Did she go with anyone at the office?"

DeeDee looked around her. "Maybe a thing," she said. "I don't know. Nothing formal."

"What do you mean, a *thing*?" Gagnon questioned.

"You know, just a thing. Two people working decide to let off a little steam. Not dating. Not seeing each other. Just…" she shrugged, "a thing."

"And that wouldn't have any repercussions? Problems at work? With spouses? Having an affair at work could cause all kinds of problems."

"No. Julia didn't have any problems." DeeDee shook her head. "I don't get where you're going with this. I thought… Julia slipped and fell. Died of hypothermia. Why are you asking all of these questions? You're making it sound like…" she trailed off.

"We're just investigating," Margie assured her. "We don't know anything. The ME has not yet made a ruling. We don't know that it was anything more than an accident."

"But it could be more. That's why you're asking."

"We don't understand what she was doing in the park. Why she would have been close to the river. We're just hoping to get the answers to some questions."

"But you're not asking any of those things. You're asking about work and affairs and jealous spouses."

"Just in case there was something more than met the eye."

DeeDee eyed them thoughtfully. "So you've buried the

lede," she suggested. "This is a much bigger investigation than you are letting on."

CHAPTER ELEVEN

*D*eeDee did her best to pry the story out of Gagnon and Margie, but they succeeded in getting out of the network offices with their secrets still intact. Margie shook her head. She had never been questioned by an investigative journalist before. Not like that. She'd certainly had reporters yell questions at her before, and had one or two interviews after a case was solved, feel-good stories outlining what they had done and that the world was a safer place now that the criminal was off the street. But being questioned by someone like DeeDee Strong was an entirely different experience. It made Margie think about the stories she'd heard of intelligence agents undergoing grueling interrogations in training so that they would be able to withstand torture if they were ever actually captured by the enemy.

DeeDee Strong would have been a great interrogator.

While there were more interviews to be done, they headed back to the office to review the surveillance footage that Siever had gone through. He was good with tech and always the first to volunteer for tedious duties like reviewing video or compiling or searching large amounts of data. Margie was relieved that he enjoyed it, as she did not, and like everyone else in the department, she was content to let Siever take charge of such tasks.

They walked by MacDonald's office on the way to the boardroom to view the video that Siever had compiled, but didn't make it without MacDonald noticing.

"Gagnon. Detectives."

They stopped and turned toward his door, exchanging looks. No one particularly wanted to fall under his scrutiny. Not when they hadn't really accomplished anything yet.

"I thought you were out doing interviews," MacDonald addressed Gagnon. "Have you made any progress?"

"We've been interviewing all morning," Gagnon confirmed. He quickly wiped his forehead, glistening with sweat, even though they had just come in from the cold. Margie hoped it was nervousness and not COVID that was giving him the sweats. He hadn't said that he was having any other symptoms.

"Any progress?"

"Not a lot, sir. Got an alibi statement for the ex-husband that seems to hold out. There are rivalries at work, but I don't get the feeling that anyone would physically assault her to get a story. But still no explanation as to why they would be at Bowness Park. Detective Siever has some surveillance video that we're just going to view."

MacDonald looked at Siever. "Does it give us a suspect?"

"Uh… not yet," Siever admitted, shifting his weight from one foot to the other. "I haven't been able to identify anyone suspicious. But I can see the victim walking into the park and part of her travels around it. She doesn't come out," he cleared his throat awkwardly, "Uh, obviously. And I don't see anyone behaving suspiciously. No one skulking around or following her but, after Gagnon and Patenaude take a look at it…"

"Do you think they'll find something you missed?"

"No. But I might have missed something. Or it might give them an idea of another direction to pursue. At any rate, we should all see exactly what happened during the last hour of her life. If we're going to solve it."

MacDonald stared at Siever for a minute. Siever swallowed and nodded, reemphasizing his words.

"Very good," MacDonald said. "We should all see it. Someone might have a brainstorm."

On MacDonald's advice, they gathered together everyone in the bullpen to watch the video surveillance that Siever had compiled. This served to make Siever anxious. He didn't like having to present to the whole room.

"Just talk to me," Margie told him as they walked to the boardroom and waited for everyone to assemble. "Don't worry about anyone else. You were going to show it to me and Gagnon, so pretend that's all you're doing. If anyone has any comments or questions, that's great. You can deal with them when they come up. That means they're engaging with what you've prepared, and that's what you want."

"And if they ask stuff that I don't know the answer to…"

Margie understood this was one of his biggest worries. They had talked about it before. "Then you just tell them that the surveillance doesn't show that, or it will have to be investigated further. No one expects you to have everything analyzed. We're just moving forward as quickly as we can on what we have gathered so far. If you hadn't pulled this together, I would have to stay late tonight, scrubbing video instead of being with my daughter, and I still wouldn't have everything pulled together like you have in the morning."

"You haven't even seen what I've done," Siever pointed out.

"I've seen it before. Your video work is always top-notch. I know it will be."

Siever smiled at this and nodded. His shoulders relaxed a little.

"You've got this," Margie told him. "You're ahead of the game, not behind."

CHAPTER TWELVE

*I*n a few minutes, everyone in the office had assembled and was waiting for the video, a couple cracking jokes about needing popcorn.

Siever looked at Margie once more, and she gave him a reassuring smile. He turned to his computer and brought the video up on the screen.

"So I found our victim entering the park through the main entrance and parking in the main lot. Her car has been identified and the crime scene techs will look at it to see if there is anything of forensic value inside the car. But we know that she drove there under her own power and that no one else was in the car with her."

They watched the video as Julia's car drove past one surveillance camera and then another angle following her farther into the parking lot. Siever had spotlighted the car so that it was clear what they were supposed to be watching. They saw Julia get out of the car, bundled up for the cold. She looked around. It was apparent that she hadn't seen anyone or anything in the parking lot that concerned her. She locked her car and walked toward one of the pathways. She hesitated, maybe unfamiliar with the terrain, but remembering instructions she had been given or what she had looked up on a map before arriving.

"I cataloged everyone who came into the park the hour ahead of her and an hour behind her," Siever said. "There is little traffic at that time of the night, so there weren't a lot of subjects to follow. Most of them are dog walkers. A few people who are just there to walk by themselves, and those are the ones I focused on."

He brought up a display that showed the best facial shot he could get of each person.

"The pictures from the surveillance camera are not good enough for facial recognition. But I followed each one across surveillance cams as much as possible, and mapped their routes around the park. People didn't generally stay for very long; it was cold. Just a half-hour walk around the park, generally, along well-marked pathways."

He brought up a map showing the routes that the various people had taken, mostly confined to the same loop.

"But that's different from our victim, who did not stick to that main loop," Siever pointed out. He brought up another map, which showed the locations of each camera that had caught Julia Louise Robertson and the implied route she had taken between them.

"There are, unfortunately, no surveillance cameras when you get off of the main trails and down to the water's edge," Siever told them. He marked the last point he had been able to catch Robertson on camera and then the point at which her body had been discovered, some distance downriver.

"I've compiled all of the video that I could get of Robertson walking through the park, as she moves from one camera to another."

There was a pause as he selected the video and then played it. As Margie had expected, his presentation was much better than she would have been able to pull together in twice as much time. Siever had managed to compile it all very professionally and had gone a lot further with it than she would have been able to, following potential suspects and mapping their routes. It was in Siever's wheelhouse. Tedious, meticulous work, all pulled into a form easily digestible by the rest of the squad.

There was not a whisper as they all watched the compiled video, watching Robertson walk from one video camera to another and then off the edge of the screen each time. Margie tried to discern everything she could from the woman's walk across the screen. She was dressed for the weather. She hadn't just gotten out of her car in Bowness Park on an impulse to relive childhood memories. She walked at a good pace. Not a slow, meandering, exploratory route, enjoying all of the wonders of nature. But not too brisk, either. She was a big woman, not in good physical shape, and she didn't move quickly enough to get out of breath.

There wasn't anyone on the surveillance tape in front of or behind her. If someone had been following her or waiting for her, he'd known enough to stay off of the camera feed. No dark shadow dogged her along the route.

"Why would she go to the river?" Jones was the first to speak after they had watched the entirety of the video compilation. "That's what I don't understand. She wasn't just there for a walk. This wasn't part of her normal routine." Jones looked at Margie and Gagnon, sitting beside Siever. "Was it? She didn't even live in the area."

"No," Margie said, "She lived in Bearspaw, a good fifteen-minute drive away, and we haven't found anyone who suggests that she went there regularly or had any kind of emotional attachment to the park. Maybe she had been there as a kid, like many of us, but no one has said anything about her going there or mentioning it recently."

"Then why? Was she meeting someone? Looking for something? Throwing something in the river?"

Margie frowned, thinking about it. She hadn't considered the possibility that Robertson had thrown something away in the river. But she hadn't been carrying anything bigger than what she might have in her pockets. And if she wanted to get rid of something that small, then surely there were plenty of places in Bearspaw where she could have thrown it away. Ponds, wells, irrigation ditches, dumpsters, forests, and open fields. There was an excess of places she could have gotten rid of something small and no one would ever have been the wiser.

Nor had she gone there to pick something up. What? A river rock? There was nothing in the park that an investigative reporter would have been interested in.

Years before, Bowness Park had been a center of social entertainment in both the summer and the winter. It had boasted a midway, with a carousel, Ferris wheel, and other rides, a dancing hall and restaurant, boating, cabins, playgrounds, a zip line and, of course, skating in the winter. But most of that was gone now. Now, it was mostly just a natural park. The restaurant, picnic areas, and playgrounds remained, but there was little to do in the winter other than skating on the lagoon and walking around the pathways. Margie could think of nothing that would have attracted Robertson to the river's edge.

CHAPTER THIRTEEN

*S*he had to be meeting with someone," Margie posited. "What else would she have been there for? It wasn't her normal stomping grounds. There was nothing to do. She didn't stay on the loops everyone else did. She must have been there to meet someone."

"But she didn't," Siever insisted, motioning to the screen. He pulled up the routes that the non-dog-walkers had taken. "These are the routes taken by those who were closest to the river, where Robertson deviated from the main trails. And the timing just doesn't allow for any of them to have met her. I recorded the time that they passed each surveillance camera, and they didn't have enough time to leave the routes I marked. They were all walking at a consistent pace, with only minor variations of a minute or two."

"What if someone had been waiting for her for over an hour?" Cruz suggested.

Siever looked at him. "It's possible," he said, "but do you really think someone was standing around out there for more than an hour? It was cold. And if someone had set up a meeting with her, why would they arrange it so that they had to wait for her outside for more than an hour? Maybe they'd make it so that *she* had to wait longer, but why would he make himself wait out in the cold for that long?"

Cruz shrugged. "Just spitballing."

Siever nodded. "It's possible, but in my experience, people don't like to stand out in the cold for longer than an hour."

There were some chuckles around the room.

"Any other thoughts?" MacDonald prodded.

"A boat in the river? A helicopter? Ski-Doo? Someone hiking in from somewhere other than the main entrance? Down the river on skis?" Margie tried to think of as many different possibilities as she could. None of them seemed too likely.

No one around the table took any of them up as being likely. Siever shook his head but didn't say anything.

"There were ski and Ski-Doo tracks along the river," Gagnon said eventually. "That's always a possibility. But there's no way to verify if someone came in that way. No cameras."

"We could check traffic cams," Margie suggested. "See if there are any on the bridge that capture part of the river. It's a long shot, but if we can see someone coming or going around the time that Robertson was there…"

Siever pursed his lips and nodded. "I'll get footage, but I don't think anything captures the river. And it wouldn't be close. Someone on the bridge saw her caught up on the log, but that's downstream from where she went in. She was carried there by the river."

"And there's no evidence we could use where she went into the river?" Cruz suggested. "Footprints? Those ski tracks? Do we have a clear indicator of her going into the water intentionally, accidentally, or at someone else's hands?"

Margie and Gagnon shook their heads.

"There is a mess of tracks in the snow on top of the ice," Gagnon said. "Lots of animals going down to drink, some human footprints or ski tracks. Nothing that is identifiable as the victim's boots, nothing that clearly identifies the point where she went into the water. Forensics did their best to narrow it down, but...?" He shrugged. "No luck. The ice may have broken under her weight and taken any evidence of what happened into the river with her. An accident, if that was what happened." He looked sideways at Margie. "And our best Indian tracker wasn't any more helpful."

Margie snorted. There were a few snickers around the table, but no one knew whether they should laugh at the politically incorrect joke. Margie called Gagnon a name she normally didn't use at the office and moved on. She had already been branded overly sensitive about comments that had been made about Indigenous people in other investigations. There was no point in telling him that he was making a racist joke when he already knew it. She had been open about her heritage with him, about their shared language base, and maybe it was his clumsy attempt to connect with her through a joke, as men often did.

"I have to say, from all of the work that Siever has done, it looks like an accident," she said to the room. "We'll make sure that the medical examiner gets a chance to review it as well, to take into consideration in his findings. The only thing that makes me hesitant to call it an accident is that I can't figure out *why* she went there in the first place. Why go to the river? Why go to Bowness Park? If I had a satisfactory answer to that question, maybe I would be satisfied with it being an accident."

MacDonald nodded briskly. "Yes. That all makes sense," he agreed. "How have the interviews so far gone? Anything interesting? Any indication that she was suicidal or having problems with someone?"

Margie looked to Gagnon to answer the question. He was the lead, after all, and she had just shared her opinion.

"Not much joy," Gagnon filled in. "There are definitely jealousies and rivalries to be considered. Her ex is violent, but his alibi seems solid, and it is doubtful that he would hire anyone to kill her after the divorce was finalized. She earned quite a bit more money than he did, so I assume if there was any alimony, she was paying him. No reason to kill the golden goose, unless he happened to know that he was named as a beneficiary in her will."

"And I doubt if he was," Margie contributed.

Gagnon nodded his agreement. "At the office, there was a lot of rivalry. It has been referred to more than once as being a cutthroat business. But then, her throat wasn't cut." This joke fell flat, no one even smiling at it. "There is a lot of competition for stories. Even her self-professed best friend was a rival, trying to beat her out for the biggest investigations. I don't get the feeling that any of them would actually do violence to get the better story, but we have all seen cases where rivalry has gotten the better of people in unbelievable ways. Soccer moms killing other players. Kids killing other kids for toys or treats, or just because they were a teacher's favorite. So I don't *see* any real motive, but sometimes…"

Margie had to agree that it was a possibility, but a doubtful one. "We could see whether any other reporters at the network live in the Bowness area."

Gagnon nodded unenthusiastically. "Might be worth it on an outside chance."

"Anything else?" MacDonald asked. "Any leads on the stories she was working on?"

"Oh, her friend at the office said she thought it was some financial scam in Manitoba. But she didn't have any details. Worth following up on. Did we get her laptop?"

"Got it this afternoon," Siever advised. "The techs haven't sent me anything yet. Once they have, I'll see what the most recent documents created or modified were. And I'll see if there is anything in Manitoba."

"Winnipeg, she thought," Margie advised, "but she wasn't sure."

"Okay," MacDonald said, in his "wrapping it up" voice. "We've all got information to follow up on. Please keep talking to her family and friends. Following up on her cases and anything on the computer. I think Bowness Park itself is a dead end. Unless we get some additional footage that we don't already have. Any current boyfriends? Girlfriends?"

"She might have had office romances," Margie told him. "I don't have any names, but it sounds like it was a pretty common occurrence with people working late. DeeDee said that she didn't have anyone steady. The occasional date, but nothing that ever went anywhere. Nothing past a date or two."

"Dating apps?" Siever asked.

"I don't know. Maybe. Did you get her phone?"

"No phone on the body or in the stuff they brought back from her house. Probably in her purse at the bottom of the river now."

"Well, you could see if you can find anything on the computer about a dating site. Most of them are on your phone these days, but she might have a site she could access from both, or there might be something in her email or messenger service that tells us if she was using one or what profiles she had looked at or connected with."

Siever nodded. She probably didn't need to tell him what to look for; he was better with the tech than she was.

"Other family or friends?" MacDonald asked. "Neighbors? They found a neighbor with a key to get into her place. Might be worthwhile to follow up with her to see if she noticed anyone new visiting the victim or hanging around the neigh-borhood lately."

"Got it," Margie agreed, jotting down a note. Bearspaw was out of her way, but maybe she could then pick up some ice cream at MacKay's in Cochrane to take home to Christina. They would both enjoy that.

CHAPTER FOURTEEN

The homicide team moved cases forward as quickly as possible, but things did not always move as quickly as they would have liked. There were many times when they were stuck waiting for tests to come in, witnesses to call them back, or for something to just fall into their laps when a case was not going well. And as other cases came along, they pushed the previous cases aside, as they diminished in urgency every day.

The press and politicians kept Julia Louise Robertson's case in the forefront as much as possible. Margie kept an eye on the media and was still seeing front-page articles on Robertson, even though they really hadn't found anything worthy of reporting.

There were memorial articles. Remembering all that she had done in the community, which, as far as Margie could tell, wasn't very much, but they were trying to make it sound like more than it was. Remembering the big breaks she had made, the stories that she had broken that changed the world or, at least, some small corner of it. Timelines showing the milestones in her life. They omitted milestones like getting married and divorced, but included birth, graduation, earning the letters behind her name, first article published, and first nomination for a Pulitzer.

Julia had lived an eventful life. Until she had shown up caught on a log in the Bow River.

They were still trying to crack the files on her computer. The drive was encrypted, which made it difficult to access the files she had written, even though they were able to make a copy of her drive and access the files without a login.

Margie wasn't sure where to begin making inquiries in Manitoba. But she had come from there and had contacts she could call upon. If Robertson were investigating a financial scheme in Manitoba, then it stood to reason that the Financial Crimes Unit of the Winnipeg Police Service might know something about it.

She tried Bud Webber, a mentor of Margie's, someone who had helped her get into law enforcement and kept an eye on her while she had been in Manitoba, making sure that she was getting along all right.

"Margie!" Bud was delighted when he heard who was calling. "Or should I say, Parks Pat?"

"Oh, you heard about that, did you?"

"Google Alerts still sends me all the clippings," he advised. "Any time your name is in the news, I read about it."

Margie's cheeks warmed. She hadn't thought about Bud following her career from such a distance.

"Well... I guess I don't need to catch you up, then," she chuckled. "I'm on a new case, and this one could have a connection with Manitoba, so I thought I would start with you, and see if you've heard anything. If you can point me in the right direction."

"Well, you know I will help if I can."

"I don't have much to go on. Just that an investigative journalist, Julia Louise Robertson, was looking into some kind of financial scheme in Manitoba. Probably Winnipeg."

He waited for more.

"That's about it," Margie said uncomfortably. "I don't know much more than that. She's a big name, so it isn't going to be about something small. It would be something pretty important or far-reaching. Maybe... I don't know. Maybe organized crime? Financial market manipulation? Something in the millions."

"That's not much to go on," Bud said, "and most of it is guesses."

"Yeah. I know. I didn't know where to start, so I called you. Maybe you can ask a few of your colleagues. See if they know a new player in town or some big deal going down soon. Or if anyone has been making inquiries. Maybe Robertson called the Financial Crimes Unit to make initial inquiries. Or tried to get access to certain documents or files."

"Well, it's possible. I'll ask around, but I'm not sure I'll be able to help you."

"I appreciate that you're even willing to try with how little I have. I wish I could give you more. I'll keep digging. We're trying to access her digital files, but they are encrypted. And I have her notepad, but it is mostly in shorthand, just using single initials for people's names and cryptic comments that don't lead us anywhere."

"You might want to scan that and send it to me. You never know; it might trigger something if it is related to a case that someone is working on."

"Okay, I'll see what I can do."

Of course, Margie had to be careful where she sent copies of documents that were evidence, and she would be sure to get MacDonald's permission first. Still, there wasn't usually a problem with sending it to someone else in law enforcement so that they could collaborate.

"And how is your family?" Bud asked before Margie could say goodbye. "Everybody keeping well?"

"I haven't talked much to anyone in Winnipeg," Margie admitted. She felt guilty about how she had left them behind and rarely even emailed or called. But she had her own life in Calgary and she had done her best to keep Christina away from any of the old influences. And some of those influences had been extended family members.

"And Christina?"

"Christina's doing really well. She's organized an Indigenous Fair at school here, and I think it will be a great event."

"How old is she now?"

"Sixteen."

"How quickly they grow up. I remember bouncing her on my knee." Bud paused. "I remember bouncing *you* on my knee!"

"Yeah, but I was twenty-five," Margie joked.

He guffawed. "Oh, I miss you. It's nice to hear from you again, even if it is just to try to squeeze information out of me like a ripe fruit and then throw me away."

"I'm not doing that. I just... well, you're the first one I thought of who might be able to give me some guidance. You've always been very helpful," she cajoled.

"You know you can call me for help any time. Even if I can't help you, I'll at least try."

"I appreciate it. You'll let me know as soon as you hear anything that might be helpful? There's a lot of pressure on this case, with the victim being something of a celebrity."

"I'll let you know the moment I hear anything," he agreed.

CHAPTER FIFTEEN

I think I saw something out on the ice that day."

Margie played the message back once more, listening for any special accent or inflection, any indication of who might have left the message. Whether it was someone she had previously spoken to. If the caller really had new information, or it was just a hoax or someone who wanted attention. The caller had not left any contact number. When they traced it, they would probably find that it came from a public phone that a number of people had access to. An airport or hotel courtesy phone, an office phone in a company that employed 3,000 people. People generally knew now that even if they told their cellphones not to display their caller ID, the police could still track a call back to the owner of the phone.

"Is it someone you know?" Gagnon asked impatiently.

"No, I don't think so. Doesn't sound like anyone we interviewed. Siever identified a few of the people from the surveillance video. It could be one of them."

"But then why not just tell us they saw something when we call them? It doesn't make sense to hold back in person and then call and leave a message like that."

"Since when do people make sense? I agree, though. I think it's probably someone who has been reading about the investigation in the news. Whether they actually know anything or not is doubtful. But they'll have to leave a number to call back if they want to talk to us."

Gagnon nodded his agreement. "Well, we'll see whether it can be traced back to a number we can reach. Probably just some crank."

Margie nodded.

Her phone rang, making her jump. Was it the anonymous witness calling back? Maybe with the realization that he had not left a number where he could be reached? But when she glanced at the display, she saw that it was Sergeant MacDonald. She picked it up.

"Yes, sir?"

"Can I see you for a moment, Patenaude? In my office?"

"Sure. I'll be right there."

"Gagnon too, if he's out there."

"He is. We'll both be right there."

Margie looked at Gagnon, who had undoubtedly seen MacDonald's name on the display. He nodded, and they walked across the bullpen to MacDonald's office.

The door was open and, when Margie reached up to knock on the frame, he looked up from his paperwork and motioned for them to come in.

"Come, come."

"What's up?" Margie asked, once they were stationed in front of him.

He seemed distracted or irritated, shuffling through a few of the stacks of paper on his desk without really looking at them and then dropping them in a pile with a thump.

"How is the progress on the Robertson case?"

"Not much," Gagnon said. "Not really anything new since this morning's briefing. We received a call from someone saying they saw what happened, but no number and obviously if she saw what happened to Robertson, she has to tell us about it before we can do anything."

MacDonald nodded. His eyes flicked to Margie, but she didn't have anything to add.

"I understand that you have been stirring things up in Winnipeg."

"Stirring things up?" Margie repeated. She thought about the few discreet calls she had made to law enforcement officers with whom she had a personal relationship. None of them had complained, and none had come up with anything that had assisted their investigation.

"We've been asked to back off. Stop calling law enforcement in Winnipeg and keep our investigation focused on Calgary. This is where she died. This is where we are going to find the clues. Or not, as the case may be."

"Who complained?" Margie asked. "I didn't know anyone was upset about it."

"I don't know. I don't get the whole story; I'm just told to stop making waves. That they don't want us messing up their investigations in Winnipeg. Whatever happened to Robertson happened to her here."

"Had she been to Winnipeg recently?" Margie asked, finding his wording curious.

"Not that I'm aware of. But everything to do with this case seems confined to Calgary, so let's keep it the focus of our investigation."

Margie shook her head. "It has been our focus... but Robertson's next big story was supposed to be from Winnipeg, so that's what I have been inquiring about."

"You have any details about what that story was?"

"Just that it was something financial, that it was based in Winnipeg or Manitoba. I've just been checking in with a few LEOs I know to see if they're aware of anything or if

Robertson had reached out to them for information or confirmation."

She had already explained all of this to MacDonald earlier, but he seemed to have forgotten those conversations or decided they were unimportant. She wasn't *trying* to cause any trouble.

He tapped his pen on the top of the desk. "Well, you've made your inquiries, and nothing has come from it, so let's drop that line of investigation and stay focused on Calgary. Maybe this anonymous caller will have something."

"We'll do our best to trace her," Margie assured him. She wondered if he would just gloss over her answer and not notice that she hadn't agreed to the rest. She was responsible for following up on all leads, whether they were in Calgary or another jurisdiction.

"Good," MacDonald approved. "I think that after that… we'll have exhausted most of the leads. OCME is leaning toward classifying it as an accident, so I think that will be the end of it. Once the manner of death is determined to be an accident, there isn't much more we can do."

"No, sir," Margie and Gagnon agreed together.

She wondered if Gagnon felt as off-balance after hearing MacDonald's instructions as she did. A tight knot in her gut told her that Robertson's death wasn't a simple accident. Why had she been out on the ice? Margie wouldn't have gone out there. And she wasn't a big woman like Robertson. Surely Robertson would have recognized the danger of getting too close to the edge of the ice, where it thinned out. She wouldn't be there for no reason.

And if the anonymous witness did know something, then there had been something to see. Was she going to claim that it had been suicide? Margie really couldn't see anyone in their right mind deciding that drowning in icy water would be a peaceful, easy way to go.

But then, someone who would do such a thing obviously wasn't in their right mind.

MacDonald shuffled a few more packets of paper.

"That's all," he snapped. "You're dismissed."

Margie and Gagnon both nodded and retreated from his office. Gagnon stopped at Margie's desk, his brows drawn down.

"What was that all about?"

"I don't know," Margie said, shaking her head. "I guess I got on someone's nerves with my calls, but it isn't like I've been making a lot of them or keep calling back to harass them. I certainly haven't made any accusations."

"Have you found out anything in Winnipeg? Even a hint?"

"No. Nothing."

It was all just a dead end.

Or that's what Margie thought.

CHAPTER SIXTEEN

*M*argie was almost falling asleep in front of the TV. Christina, leaning against her, was also slack and breathing heavily. The two of them were certainly a pair.

Her phone vibrated in her pocket, making Margie jolt awake. She looked first at the TV to see what was on and to mute it so that it wouldn't interfere with the call. Then she looked at the phone screen.

Bud Webber. She smiled and swiped to answer the call.

"Bud, how are you?" she asked warmly.

She looked at Christina to see if she were awake and to tell her who it was, so she could say 'hi' to an old friend, but Christina's head was tipped back and she breathed heavily.

"I've been looking at the notebook you sent me."

"Oh, was that helpful?" Margie perked up a bit at that. She hadn't found anything in the notebook that had been at all enlightening to her, but maybe something had caught Bud's eye that meant something to him.

"Actually… yes, possibly. I might have a connection for you."

"What was it?"

"The key was on that last page you sent to me."

"Encounter with iceberg?" Margie asked, laughing. It was such a strange headline for Robertson to write about, especially if it were related to Manitoba. It had stuck in her mind. Obviously, there were no icebergs in the landlocked prairie province. It wasn't like it was Newfoundland, which had a rich history of iceberg encounters.

"Yes," Bud said. "Encounter with iceberg."

"Okay. That meant something to you?" Maybe iceberg was a code name for a police operation in Winnipeg. Most police departments gave undercover operations names that were randomly generated and had absolutely nothing to do with the operation itself. It could be Operation Stapler or Operation Magpie.

Or Operation Iceberg.

"You said that you thought your reporter's investigation could somehow be related to finance."

"Yes."

"Iceberg is the nickname of a Russian mobster."

Margie caught her breath. Her heart rate quickened.

"Really?"

That could be it. A meeting with a mobster. Not a boat running into an iceberg like the Titanic. Not the very tip of a huge operation that was mostly hidden from sight.

A person. A meeting with a real person.

"Tell me about this mobster," she told Bud, her voice hoarse.

"Okay... his name is Victor Petrov. Born and bred in Winnipeg to an immigrant family. Into a poor Russian-Canadian community. His family wasn't anything to speak of in the mob. Maybe they had some distant connections. Maybe they'd done some messengering or muling for the organization, but nothing that was big or important enough for them to be arrested and connected to the mob."

"Yeah." Margie looked for a piece of paper to jot some notes on, having already changed out of her work clothes and left her duty notepad in the bedroom. She laid her hands instead on Christina's laptop and, after a glance at her still snoozing away, opened it up and started a new document.

Bud went on. "Victor himself did get involved with the mob as a street-level soldier and worked his way up through the ranks. He's smart. Ruthless. Good at flying under law enforcement's radar. We hear things about him, but no one ever has the proof to nail him."

"No convictions?"

"A few for low-level stuff. And some arrests that never led to anything. I've suspected more than once that he had some connections *inside* law enforcement. I have no proof of that or any way to know what organizations he might have his feelers into. I'm talking to you unofficially. You can bet that I will not be making a report that I've passed anything on to you."

Margie breathed slowly, trying to calm her rapidly beating heart. "This is it. This is who Robertson was investigating."

"It's possible," Bud agreed cautiously. "I wouldn't swear to it, but you don't see a lot of icebergs in Manitoba."

"What's with the name?" she laughed. "Why Iceberg?"

"Cold as ice. A lot more dangerous than he looks."

"What does he look like? Can you send me a picture?"

"I'm sure you can get something on your end. I don't want to be connected to your investigation. You found this yourself. You searched the databases for a criminal with the known nickname of Iceberg."

Margie could do that. Had she realized that Iceberg was a person rather than part of an interesting headline then, of course, she would have searched the criminal databases for him. And now she would.

"Sure, of course. I'll do that. Does he have any connections with Calgary? Why would he have been here?"

"I don't know if he was, or if he sent someone else to take care of the problem. All I can gather from your victim's notebook is that she was supposed to be meeting with someone, whether it was Petrov himself or a witness who was going to tell her about a meeting he'd had with Petrov. And during that meeting, she ended up in the water."

"Would she have been a danger to him? How much could she have had on him? If the police could never get anything on him, what are the chances that a reporter could have uncovered enough to worry him?"

"You've seen some of these exposés on TV. People will talk to reporters when they won't talk to the police. And they're very good at what they do. Your victim was at the top of the game. She'd produced some really good stuff in the past. If he'd even gotten wind of the fact that she was investigating him, then I don't think it would matter if she had anything on him yet. He would want to get her out of the way."

Margie nodded slowly. She typed notes into Christina's computer, her mind racing, trying to get down all of the information Bud had given her and to make lists of the things she would need to investigate on her own.

"You need to keep this quiet," Bud warned again. "You don't want to attract attention to yourself, and if he's got people inside the police department, they may be notified when you access Petrov's records. You're going to need to make it look routine. You just happened to run his records because of the word iceberg, but once you looked at his files, you didn't think there was anything there. You discounted him because he's in Manitoba and you can't connect him to Calgary."

Margie was already keeping her continued investigation into any Manitoba connections quiet. It would be easy enough to say that once she saw that Petrov was in Manitoba, she backed off because her sergeant had already told her to stop investigating any Manitoba connections. There was no Calgary connection, so she didn't pursue it any further—an abandoned investigative angle.

If she were lucky, maybe there was more than one criminal with the alias of Iceberg, and she could spend more time on the other one. Bury her interest in Victor Petrov.

"Be careful," Bud emphasized.

"I will."

"I don't want to hear that something has happened to you. I would never forgive myself."

"I really appreciate you bringing this to me. I'll be careful. Nothing is going to happen."

"You think about your little girl. You want her to have to grow up without a mother?"

Margie put her arm around her sleeping "little girl," already taller than she was and champing at the bit for more independence. However much Christina thought that she was ready for the adult world, Margie did not want her living the rest of her life without a mother. Margie herself had cut off most of her contact with her own mother at Christina's age, and living in the adult world had been much more difficult than she had ever anticipated.

"I'm not going to let anything happen to Christina. Including losing her mother," she assured Bud. "Thank you for the warning. I'll be careful."

He gave a heavy sigh. "I'm already regretting telling you. I should have just stayed out of it. If Petrov is your guy... I wish we could just leave him for someone else to take down."

"Well, I'm not the lead on the case. If we do end up being able to connect him to Robertson's death, my name doesn't have to come into it." Was she throwing Gagnon under the bus? Did that mean that some shadowy figure from Manitoba or the depths of the police department would come after him?

"And Petrov's name isn't going to come up unless we have something solid on him. Something we can arrest him for. Otherwise, it will just be one search I did for an alias in the course of the investigation."

"You make sure of it."

"I will."

CHAPTER SEVENTEEN

*M*argie rubbed her eyes and considered whether to take a break, go for a walk and get some lunch, or grab another cup of coffee from the breakroom, hoping that the caffeine would give her the boost she needed.

It had been a long week. She had officially relegated the Robertson case to second place while she and Cruz reactivated a series of youth gang deaths as threats of further gang violence had been heard over ALERT's informant networks. If they could find some information that the original investigation hadn't managed to turn up, maybe they could grab up the culprits and prevent further unnecessary deaths. She always hated it when she knew that teens were at risk. She couldn't help thinking about Christina and her friends. Even though they were not involved in any gang stuff—and Margie had her eyes open and was sure they were not—she knew that innocent children were never truly safe. There had been some tragic deaths of bystanders who had happened to get caught in the crossfire. No one was safe from gang violence and, if it went down at the schools, a lot of innocent people were at risk.

And that meant that her investigation of the Robertson

case had to go on the back burner. As far as anyone knew, there wasn't any risk of additional deaths on the file. Not as far as Gagnon or MacDonald were concerned. They were both of the opinion that it had just been a bizarre accident. Only Margie thought it might be a homicide. She kept her inquiries to after-hours and tried to keep it below the radar of the rest of the department. She couldn't use the work servers and databases without leaving a trail. Still, she could do public records searches, internet research, and phone calls in the evening without anyone being aware.

But that meant she was putting in much longer hours than usual, which was wearing on her physically.

Not only that, but Christina's Indigenous Fair was coming up quickly. Margie had agreed to make bannock and to talk with the students about Indigenous people and law enforcement.

Moushoom would also participate, telling old stories, talking about his time learning from his parents and elders, in residential school, and then trying to reconcile the two worlds and find his place in them. He would talk about the things he had grown up with—hunting and foraging, eating bannock, wearing and using a Métis sash, and the other traditional practices. Margie would need to transport him from the nursing home to the school. It was going to be a very busy day.

So she was not just tired out by the double duty she had been doing as a detective, but also with preparing her presentations and helping Christina make all of the final arrangements for the fair. It was sometimes hard to get the members of her community to show up at the expected time. They tended to have a looser interpretation of "on time." Margie gave Christina as much helpful advice as she could on how to get people to show up for the presentation slots they had been assigned.

She elected for another cup of coffee. A walk would have to

wait. Siever was in the breakroom when she refilled her mug. Margie paused, thinking about the work she had been doing.

Things had been pretty quiet over the last week or two. Everyone seemed to have forgotten about the Robertson case. Maybe she could do a little work from the police servers and make some progress.

"Hey, Siever…"

He stirred creamer into his coffee, looking intent. After a minute, he looked at her and flicked his stir stick into the garbage.

"Eh? What?"

"I was wondering. You know all of that footage that we have of Bowness Park?"

He blinked, considering. "You mean for the Robertson case?" he asked finally, making it sound like it had taken place fifty years ago.

"Yeah."

He shrugged. "Okay, sure. Yeah, we have lots of footage. Not that it did us any good."

"If I had a face, would you be able to find some time to look through some of the surveillance video to see if he shows up?"

"Yeah, sure." He took a sip of his coffee. "I didn't know we had a suspect."

"Well… let's say a person of interest. Maybe not even that right now. Just a hunch. Not even something that we are ready to put down on paper. But if you could spend a few minutes looking at video…"

"It would take more than a few minutes," he pointed out. "There are hours of video."

"Well, yes. But not all of it shows faces. You would only need to review footage that shows faces. And from what I remember, only a couple of cameras tended to catch people's faces as they arrived or left."

"Yeah." He shrugged. "I can find some time. I don't know how long it will take, and it won't be top priority."

"No. I wouldn't want you to spend a lot of time, or to let anyone know that you were working on it."

He didn't ask her why. Any other detective would have either asked or given her a knowing look, understanding that she was pursuing something she wasn't supposed to. But Siever just nodded and accepted this.

"Sure. Just send me the picture."

"Thanks. I appreciate it."

Margie hadn't been able to find anything showing that Petrov had flown from Winnipeg to Calgary. No known aliases had been used to book a commercial flight. But that didn't mean that he hadn't used a private plane. Or driven from Winnipeg to Calgary, as Margie and Christina had done. It was a thirteen-hour drive without breaks, but it was doable. She couldn't imagine a mobster choosing to drive instead of flying, but he wouldn't necessarily have done the driving himself. There were bound to be plenty of underlings to do that kind of thing. Petrov could sit in the back of a limo with his computer or TV and be perfectly comfortable with a couple of well-timed breaks.

He could still have been in Calgary the day that Robertson had died. The only way they could know if he had been in Bowness Park that day was to find him on the security video.

Margie's phone rang as she returned to her desk with her coffee. The coffee had been made some time ago by the smell of it, and she wasn't sure whether she could actually stomach it. But she hadn't wanted to take the time to make a fresh pot.

She picked up the phone without looking at the caller ID.

"Patenaude."

"Oh, is this Detective Patenaude?" a woman's voice asked pleasantly.

Margie rolled her eyes. She wasn't sure why people had to

ask when she had just said her name. It wasn't like they couldn't understand what she said.

"Yes, this is Detective Patenaude. How can I help you?"

"This is Estelle Sinclair from the mayor's office…"

Margie thought that Estelle expected her to recognize her name, but it wasn't someone she had dealt with before. And it wasn't like she dealt with the mayor's office very often. That was above her pay grade.

"Yes?" she asked, clipped.

"I wonder if you and I could get together for a few minutes for a chat."

"Can I ask what this is about?"

"It's about a case that you are working on." There was a pause and, when Margie didn't jump in to guess what case it was, she went on in a tentative tone. "The Robertson file?"

"Oh? Do you have information on the Robertson file?" Margie asked. Where did Estelle think she was going with this? Their anonymous witness had never called back, maybe deciding it was too dangerous to talk to the police. But Margie didn't think it had been Estelle's voice on the voicemail message. Though, of course, she might always have been trying to disguise it, speaking in a lower register than usual.

"I would like to talk to you about it," Estelle told her, not clarifying.

"Well, I suppose, but I am working on other files with a higher priority right now. Maybe you and I could get together after the Christmas break…"

"We need to talk today."

"Today? This is a low-priority file. I don't think I can get together on it today."

"Did you hear me tell you I'm with the mayor's office? I think you might want to reconsider."

Margie sat down in her chair. She looked at the caller ID on the phone to ensure that it did say City of Calgary on it. A lot of crackpots might be running around saying that they were with the mayor's office. She wasn't going to meet with all of them.

"Can you tell me why the urgency?"

"I will discuss that when we meet."

Maybe they were going to issue some statement on the status of the file. Maybe Robertson's extended family was pressuring for some resolution, or at least an update statement. Robertson had been an important person in some circles. Influential. They didn't want it to look like they had forgotten about her. The city might want to name some scholarship after her. Or a piece of public art or a memorial marker.

"I supposed I could give you a few minutes this afternoon," she agreed finally. "When can you be here?"

She was pretty sure that Estelle would turn around and tell her that the meeting needed to be done at the City of Calgary offices, and however quickly Margie was able to get there would be just fine. But Estelle surprised her.

"I don't want this meeting to be at your offices or mine," she said firmly. "A private room… maybe at the Pete Club?"

"Uh… okay. You can get one for us?"

"Of course," Estelle agreed. "If you want to head over there now…"

"Now?"

"I'll get a room reserved and be over there before you. If you could grab a cab and get over there as quickly as possible…"

Margie blew out her breath in disbelief. Who did this woman think she was to just be ordering a homicide officer to drop everything she was doing and get over to a meeting?

She wasn't even the lead investigator on the Robertson case. It was Gagnon's case.

"Detective?" Estelle prompted.

"Okay. But I expect you to tell me why it was so urgent when I get there."

"I'm sure you will understand."

Margie looked at the papers she had spread out over her desk. So much for the advent of the paperless office. "I'll get there as soon as I can."

"Thank you, Detective."

Margie shrugged and hung up. She took a few minutes to sort through the papers on her desk and get them neatly compiled and locked up so that she would be able to pick up where she had left off later.

CHAPTER EIGHTEEN

*M*argie doubted that she would get reimbursement for a cab to the Pete Club, but she called one anyway. She didn't want to spend her time driving around the downtown core looking for the Pete Club and then looking for parking nearby. If she did find parking, it would be as expensive as taking a cab anyway.

She went in the nondescript entrance to the Petroleum Club and found herself in a plush lobby. She had no idea where to go. She approached the reception desk, and a woman with a snowy white mask snapped to attention and leaned forward to engage with her, immediately helpful.

"Are you meeting somewhere here today?"

"I… yes. Umm, Estelle from the Mayor's office. What was her last name…" Margie tried to recall it, patting her pockets for her notepad or phone. She must have written it down on one of them.

"Estelle Sinclair is waiting for you in the Shaunavon Room. I will have someone escort you there. One moment."

Margie was escorted to the room by a dark-suited, masked man who said nothing, but nodded politely to her. The Shaunavon Room turned out to be a bright, airy room with a table and chairs and coffee service waiting, along with a pinched-looking dark-haired woman who had to be Estelle.

"Ah, Detective Patenaude." Estelle stood up to greet her, then decided not to shake hands and sat down again, motioning for Margie to sit across from her.

"Help yourself to a cup of coffee."

Unsurprisingly, it was much fresher and of much better quality than the coffee from the breakroom, which Margie had dumped down the drain. Margie helped herself and sat down.

"So, can you tell me exactly what this is about?"

Estelle screwed up her face like she had bitten into a lemon. Maybe Margie should have eased into the conversation more diplomatically, but she didn't have the time to play politics with the mayor's office. She sat back and waited for Estelle's response.

"We have tried to reach out before to address issues of... resources being put into avenues of investigation which are not... profitable."

Margie frowned, taking a moment to consider Estelle's response. "Yes...?"

"I believe you are still pursuing a Manitoba connection with Julia Louise Robertson's unfortunate death."

"No," Margie said flatly. There was no way for Estelle's office to know who she was talking to or what inquiries she was making when she was away from her office computer and the police department servers. Unless they had her home network bugged or tracked, which Margie thought was extremely unlikely. The mayor's office didn't have that kind of money or technology. If they felt that she was still pursuing a Manitoba connection, it was just a guess.

Estelle looked taken aback at the flat denial. "Really. I understand you're from Manitoba, so, understandably, you were interested in the possibility of a connection with your home province."

"Uh-huh. I think I told you on the phone that the Robertson investigation is lower on my list right now. There isn't much we can do to prove that she died one way or another. Unfortunately, we've run out most of our leads and it's going cold."

Estelle nodded, but looked unconvinced.

"You still have family in Manitoba, don't you? Family and friends?"

"Yes." Margie swallowed. She waited for Estelle to warn her off, to tell her that if she continued to work off-books on the Robertson file, things would happen to people she knew and loved. Bud had warned her about this. He had warned her that Petrov had connections and that if Margie left any trail, they would know about it and retaliate.

Who had they talked to? How much did they know and how much were they just being cautious and trying to keep her from becoming a problem?

"You must miss them," Estelle said. "Even with all of the communication methods available to us right now, it's not the same as having dinner together. Dropping in on friends or loved ones for a chat. And your people have such a strong sense of community."

Which was both true and not true. There was a strong Métis community, both in Winnipeg and in Calgary. But Margie's immediate family had not been a part of her life since she had become pregnant with Christina. And that was a long time ago. It had been a relief to leave Winnipeg behind and to reconnect with Moushoom, who had never said a judgmental word about her becoming pregnant so young. He adored Christina and would never say anything negative about her birth or existence.

Estelle swirled her drink, which was not coffee, but a glass of ice and clear liquid. Water or liquor? Margie felt cold just looking at it.

Ice.

Iceberg.

Icy water.

She tried not to think about Robertson's death and how she must have felt in those last few minutes or seconds of her life. How long had she been conscious? How long did she know she was going to die?

"I've been hearing wonderful things about this Indigenous Fair that your daughter has been organizing," Estelle commented.

Margie felt even colder, goosebumps standing up on her neck and arms.

"My daughter—my teenage daughter—has nothing to do with the investigation. Why would you bring her up?"

"I was just thinking… how nice it would be for her if the mayor made an appearance at the fair and said a few kind words about it. Maybe brought the press with him. That would be nice, wouldn't it?"

"Of course it would," Margie agreed. She knew that Christina had reached out to the mayor and other civic leaders, hoping that some of them would acknowledge the fair in some way and get it some good publicity.

"On the other hand, there are a lot of people these days who are sick of hearing about the privileges that should be afforded the Aboriginal community. This country has put billions of dollars into reparations for wrongs that were done generations ago. We keep hearing about all of the problems in the native communities. The alcoholism, drug abuse, abuse, and neglect of their children, Indigenous people killing each other. We see them all around us, drunk on the train or at bus stops, panhandling and making a nuisance of themselves. Calgarians have had enough."

Fury boiled up in Margie. She had, of course, heard it all. Estelle was right; there were plenty of people who were tired of hearing about Indigenous rights. About the lands and culture that had been stripped away from them. The genocide all across the Americas. People were tired of it and didn't hesitate to express their opinions.

"Something like that could poison this Indigenous Fair," Estelle commented. "If the wrong people showed up, if the mayor happened to say how it was a kind of racism against whites, Muslims, and Blacks in Canada. Asians, Hispanics, other immigrants. How maybe we need to stop cosseting and promoting the cause of the First Nations in Canada and start treating them the same as anyone else, not as a separate, special culture deserving of our pity and our pockets."

"The mayor would not say that," Margie asserted. "He would be lynched."

Estelle gave a little shrug.

And maybe the mayor wouldn't say anything like that. Still, perhaps he would say that he hoped other cultural groups in the school would offer similar educational opportunities about their heritage, pointing out that the focus shouldn't all be on the Indigenous cultures and that he would like to see something else. He could say something else that would encourage the closet racists to make their opinions known. Someone from his office, like Estelle, could put the word out to neo-Nazis and other groups, who would make trouble for them. Christina's event, the project she'd put her heart and soul into for weeks, would be ruined.

"So the reason you asked me to come here was to threaten me," she said, looking Estelle in the eye.

"It's not a threat. Just an observation. How easy it is for something like this to go the wrong way, especially in today's political climate."

"You think that I'm not paying attention to what I've been

told and investigating something that you don't want to be investigated, so you threaten my kid."

"*I* don't care what you investigate. You can investigate whatever you like. I have no skin in the game. I'm not your boss. I don't know what he's told you. And I don't know what you're doing." She looked at Margie, and her gaze was cunning.

Margie didn't know how she knew or guessed that Margie was still working on the Robertson case, still looking in the "wrong" direction. But she knew. And she, or someone she was connected to, wanted to put an end to it.

Someone had figured it out. There was a mole at the office, or someone had access to her internet history or phone logs. Maybe the idea of someone bugging her house wasn't as crazy as she had thought.

"So." Estelle sat back in her chair and tipped up her glass, ice cubes tinkling. She put it down on the table. "Do we have an understanding?"

"I understand you perfectly," Margie told her.

"Good." Estelle smiled. "I'm delighted to hear it."

Margie stood. "You can tell the mayor that he doesn't need to worry. I will put the Robertson case to bed. One way or another."

CHAPTER NINETEEN

*I*t was a few days before Siever got back to Margie on the surveillance video. She was so busy with other work and helping Christina with the final arrangements for the Indigenous Fair that she hardly even thought about it. There was no longer any urgency to the Robertson case, and it would be better if she put it on the back burner, at least until the Indigenous Fair was over. She could pick it up again after the Christmas break. Then, she would look at the case with fresh eyes, and maybe she would be able to identify something she had missed.

Siever stood by Margie's desk for a minute, waiting for her to finish what she was working on and look at him. Margie pushed away the file she had been staring at. Her eyes were scratchy from staring too much at the fine print and too much dust. She felt like she hadn't blinked or slept in a week. She rubbed her eyes, even though that was probably more likely to rub dust into them than to produce cleansing tears.

"Detective Siever." She held her palms cupped over her eyes. "What've you got?"

"I found him."

"What?" She uncovered her eyes. "You found who?"

"The picture you gave me. You wanted me to look through the surveillance video for the man in the picture."

"Right." Margie blinked. The picture of Petrov.

Siever had found Petrov on the surveillance video?

How had they missed it the first time? If Petrov was there to meet with Robertson and had been instrumental in her death, how had they missed it the first time they had examined the video surveillance?

"You found him?" she demanded. "You found him in Bowness Park the day that Robertson was killed?"

Siever nodded, looking smug. "I found him."

Margie swore under her breath. "Show me! I have to see this!"

He grinned at her, as delighted as a kid that she was so excited about his discovery. He bent over Margie's keyboard and navigated to the shared workspace for the Robertson file. He found the video he wanted and scrubbed through the first portion of it. Then he let it play.

Margie watched the video playing with eagle eyes. She watched people come and go from the screen, but didn't see Petrov.

"You missed him," Siever told her.

"What? I was watching. How did I miss him?"

Siever rewound it and played it again. Margie looked at each face carefully.

Siever paused the video. He pointed to a dog walker. Margie had been looking only at the lone walkers. She focused on the dog walker and Siever pressed play to restart the video. As he looked around, Margie got a good look at his face. She got out her phone and brought up the picture. She held it up while she looked at him on the video. Siever was right. It *was* Petrov. And they had missed it the first time because they had discounted the dog walkers. They had only been looking for an isolated person walking, following Robertson or preceding her into the park.

"He has a dog!"

Siever nodded. "We didn't look at the dog walkers. We assumed that anyone who met with her or did anything to harm her would have been one of the solitary walkers. A bad assumption."

"Yes," Margie agreed. She looked at the time stamp on the video. "This was before Robertson got to the park, right?"

"Yes."

"So he could have gone wherever he wanted to set up an ambush, and then given her directions to get to him."

"Yup."

"Can you follow him through the park? Establish where he went? Where he might have attacked her?"

She should have known that Siever would be prepared for this question. He brought up a map and showed her the time-stamps indicating when he had been at each camera location. And a dashed line when he was away from a trail for an extended period of time. Close to the river.

As a dog walker, he could claim that he had been letting his dog run off-leash for a while, playing a game with him so that he got proper exercise and would settle down for the night. Even if off-leash dogs were prohibited, he could shrug that off in embarrassment and admit that he had broken the rule. People did it all the time. How often had Margie gone to a leash-restricted park with Stella properly secured, and had other dogs run up to her with no leash, their humans lagging far behind? It happened all the time. Every park. At least once, if not multiple times each visit.

"He was out of camera range at the same time as Robertson," Margie commented, "Except he returned to camera and she never did."

Siever grunted and nodded.

"Somehow, he got her into the river. Attacked her and bound her? Hit her over the head and knocked her out? Pushed her into the water? Held her under?"

Siever watched her as she tried to come up with a likely solution.

"She didn't have any injuries like that," he pointed out. "No blunt force trauma. No ligatures. No bruises."

"She had some bumps and scrapes on her face."

"A few of them," he admitted.

But he was right. There was nothing to indicate a struggle. Or a knockout. Nothing to indicate how Petrov had overpowered the large woman.

A drug? Chloroform? An injection? Something he had put in her water bottle before she got there? A drink at a bar before they went to the park? Was it supposed to be some kind of assignation and he had turned on her?

But Robertson had known him as the Iceberg. That was what she had written in her notebook. She would have known where the nickname came from. That he had ice water in his veins. He was a dangerous man, even if he didn't look it. He had promised her a story, not a romantic encounter. He had convinced her that he was going to be her source. He would spill details about his criminal organization and how things worked—or didn't work—in the criminal justice system. How money was laundered, if she had only been interested in the financial fraud aspect of the organization.

Russian mob. Had Robertson really planned to meet a Russian mobster by herself, far away from anyone who could help her? Had he convinced her that he was harmless, that she had nothing to worry about? He must have a silver tongue.

Siever forwarded to the end of the surveillance video, to Petrov walking back out of the park. Margie watched him critically. Was this how a man looked after killing a woman? His walk was calm. He wasn't looking around in fear as if afraid of being caught. The Iceberg seemed as cool as his name implied.

She continued to stare at the screen after he had disappeared from sight. Another dog walker followed him. A woman with a smaller dog. She looked guiltier than Petrov. Her movements were jerky. Her eyes were wide, and she was clearly trying to act normal when something was very wrong.

An accomplice? Had the two of them been working together? Surely not. What reason would he have to align himself with an amateur? Someone who could give away the game and, by the look of her, was likely to do just that. If he had been working with her, they would have found a second body. He would have eliminated her, too.

Margie remembered the anonymous witness. The message on her voicemail.

"I think I saw something out on the ice that day."

She turned and looked at Siever.

"We need to find this woman."

CHAPTER TWENTY

*M*argie agonized for several days over what to tell Christina, if anything, about what Estelle had said. Ultimately, she decided it was better if Christina knew ahead of time. At least she would be mentally prepared if something happened at the Indigenous Fair and wouldn't be devastated.

They had gone out for pizza not that long ago, so Margie suggested A&W instead. Christina ordered a veggie burger, and they sat inside the restaurant to eat. Margie felt like it was a discussion that would be easier to have away from home.

Margie explained to Christina, as gently as she could, about the threats or warnings that had been received from Estelle, though she didn't mention the mayor's office. Margie wouldn't be surprised to discover that the mayor had no idea what Estelle was doing in his name. While Estelle might have some control over his itinerary, Margie doubted that the threat had originated from him or that Estelle could guarantee he would make either the positive or the negative comments she had suggested. But that didn't mean she couldn't target the Indigenous Fair and make sure it was a fiasco.

Christina ate her burger slowly, looking at Margie and thinking about it.

"It isn't like I haven't heard all of that before," she said finally. She seemed reluctant to disclose this to Margie. "Not everyone has been real positive about the fair."

"Well, I guess I wouldn't have expected everybody to be excited about it," Margie admitted. "Have you had a lot of negative feedback? People who don't want to see it happen, as opposed to those who are just apathetic and don't care if you do it or not?"

"Yeah. I've had threats."

"You've what?" Margie struggled to keep her voice steady. Why was this the first time she was hearing about it? She wanted to know who had made threats and where they lived. She was going to see that they were prosecuted personally.

Christina shrugged. "Don't tell me you've never been threatened before," she said.

"Well, of course, but…"

"Did you think I wouldn't be? What? Because my mom is a cop? Because I'm just so cute?"

Margie chuckled. "Well yes, two excellent reasons."

"It's gonna happen. Whether I'm pushing for Indigenous rights, education, or just riding the train. People are going to speak up. I don't like it, but most of it I can just ignore."

"Have you had… any physical harassment? Anyone putting their hands on you?"

Christina swallowed. "Not usually. And most of the time, I hang out with Tracy and others. I'm not by myself. So mostly… I can avoid it."

"You need to tell the school if you are being physically abused. That can't be allowed to continue."

"Yeah." Christina shrugged in a "That ain't gonna happen" way. "I'll keep that in mind."

"How bad has it been? I can't believe I didn't even know. Why didn't you tell me?"

"I'm a big girl, and I look after myself. It hasn't been so bad. Pushing, usually. Pulling on my braid. Grabbing my— grabbing me. You know. I can handle it."

"Oh, honey." Margie sighed and put her hand over Christina's. "I'm sorry. And I'm sorry I didn't know about it."

"It's fine, Mom. I can deal with it. And I'm not afraid of whatever these guys you were talking to do. If they want to send protesters or talk smack about the Indigenous Fair, that's just fine. Don't they say that any publicity is good publicity? They'll just bring more attention to the fair. And if it's something controversial and they get people riled up, maybe that will make our people take it more seriously. See that it is important and not just shouting into the void."

Margie allowed a small smile. "That's a good attitude," she agreed. "We can't do anything if they decide that they are going to protest it. So we'll just have to deal with whatever comes. Or you will. I doubt it will be directed at me, even though I am the person they are trying to influence."

"What don't they want you to investigate? And why not?"

"I can't say much about it. But there are organized crime connections. And maybe some powerful people leaning on politicians, or moles in law enforcement. Bad players who want to influence the outcome and make sure that I can't solve the case or get enough evidence to arrest the guy who I believe is responsible."

"Responsible for killing someone?"

"Yes."

Christina frowned. "Well, you be careful. I don't want you getting mixed up in something dangerous. If they are that concerned about what you are going to find out..."

They had been there before. A threat to send protesters to Christina's school was nothing. The real worry was their sending an enforcer or hit man to her school or their house. And if they had already bugged Margie's house, they were way past the need to find her address. She had searched for bugs once and was reasonably convinced there weren't any, but she couldn't be sure. They were getting smaller and more sophisticated all the time.

"I'll be careful," she assured Christina. "I'm not even working on it this week. We need to focus on your event. I need to review my notes again, make sure I'm ready for my presentation, and we still have a few errands to run to pick up displays."

Christina nodded and tapped her phone to get to her project plan and see what remained to be done.

CHAPTER TWENTY-ONE

*A*nd then the day arrived. Margie and Christina slept little the night before the Indigenous Fair. Both of them were checking and rechecking their lists. Margie knew that there would be hiccups. There would be latecomers and no-shows. There would be fewer kids than they expected at the event since school would let out for the Christmas break the next day. Families who wanted to get a head start on their vacations would already be gone. Kids who figured that their classes wouldn't cover anything important when people were already on vacation and who thought that the Indigenous Fair was lame would skip, going to the mall for some last-minute holiday shopping or five-finger discounts rather than school.

But it had been well planned. Christina and Tracy had worked hard on it. Margie had her talks and bannock-making demonstration prepared, as well as small bags of baked bannock ready to hand out.

There had been an article in the Calgary Herald about the planned event, and there wasn't anything negative in it. No suggestion that Indigenous people were being favored over other cultural groups or that they shouldn't be given a podium to express their grievances when so much had already been done for them. The press used all of the right words and the article had clearly been vetted for anything that could be construed as even a little bit racist.

If there were protesters, then there were protesters. That would just make the apathetic students more interested in seeing what was going on.

"I guess it's time to go get Moushoom," Margie announced, checking the time for about the fiftieth time in the last hour.

"Let's do this!" Christina agreed, and gave a nervous giggle.

They drove the route that they usually walked to get to the nursing home, and Margie parked in the loading zone in front of the building.

She had thought that she would have to go up to Moushoom's room to get him ready and bring him down, but he was waiting in front of the doors in his wheelchair, wearing his traditional garb with Métis sash proudly on display. A male nurse stood beside him, playing on his phone. He looked up from the screen when Margie pulled in front of the doors. He slid the phone into his pocket, and took the handles of the wheelchair to push Moushoom up to the car. He set the brakes and opened the car door.

"I can do it," Moushoom told the nurse when he attempted to help him into the car. He only needed to stand up and turn around to get into the car seat. He mainly needed the wheelchair when he got tired or lost his balance. He could walk short distances as long as he was not too tired.

Margie watched Moushoom carefully maneuver his body into the passenger seat. He smiled at her and the nurse.

"You see? I might be an old man, but I can still get from one place to another."

The nurse agreed. He folded the wheelchair and Christina

got out of the back seat to put it into the trunk of the car. It was a tight fit, but they had cleared everything else out of the trunk before leaving the house to ensure they would have room. Christina slammed the trunk shut and got back into the car.

"You have a good day, now," the nurse told Moushoom, shutting the car door after ensuring that Moushoom's elbow was tucked in and would not be hit by the closing door.

"How are you today?" Margie asked, twisting around to give him a hug and a quick kiss on the cheek. "Ready for some fun?"

"Who thought I would be going back to school at my age?" Moushoom joked.

"As a teacher," Christina pointed out, "not a student. You've always been a good teacher."

"We are all students, too," Moushoom told her, "even a tough old bird like me still has things to learn."

❦

THERE WERE no protesters outside the school with signs. There was no graffiti smeared across the side of the school, the cars, or chalked on the pavement. Everything seemed to be quiet. Just a typical school day. Or a quieter-than-normal school day, the parking lot only half full.

Margie found a parking space near the doors so Moushoom would not need to walk too far. There were a few other cars and trucks around filled with dancers from the various bands around Calgary in their colorful costumes, from children who were barely walking to men as old as Moushoom or older, all ready to participate in the opening of the Indigenous Fair. Margie had been worried about putting them right at the beginning, since they would have to get there early, but there were a good number of people there. Enough to keep everyone entertained, even if they happened to be missing one or two acts. The Nakoda chief doing the opening prayer stood outside his car smoking as he awaited their directions.

CHAPTER TWENTY-TWO

*B*efore Margie knew it, the fair was all finished. The dances and other presentations were done. Students had been able to go from kiosk to kiosk to see arts and crafts, study ancient artifacts, or sample traditional foods. The food had been a popular draw, of course, but the students had also sat quietly, mesmerized and not looking at their phones when Moushoom had told them stories. They were not quite as quiet and attentive for Margie's talk about law enforcement of and by Indigenous peoples, about the National Inquiry into Missing and Murdered Indigenous Women in Canada, and about her experiences in the Winnipeg and Calgary police departments. But they had been respectful, and Margie thought a few of them had been making notes on their phones during the presentation rather than texting each other.

"I am so tired!" Christina said, flopping down onto the couch. "I swear, I'm going to sleep for three days."

"Well, you can if you need to," Margie agreed. She and Christina would have Friday, Saturday, and Sunday to relax and recover. Days when she didn't have to do anything else if she didn't want to. Maybe turn on a couple of Christmas specials on the TV and veg out eating leftover bannock. Then, on Monday, Margie would return to work, getting in a few more days before Christmas.

The time between Christmas and New Year's was always a busy time for the homicide unit. Stresses were high, money was short, family members were together who normally couldn't stand each other. Depressives who had made it through Christmas for the sake of their families gave up and tried to slip quietly away. And then there was the drinking. Alcohol flowed freely at family dinners, get-togethers of friends who lived or went to school in other cities, and widowers and singles trying to numb the pain of loneliness. Almost without fail, New Year's Eve or Day would kick off the year with a hit-and-run, a gang shooting, or some other death for the department to investigate. New Year's was not a holiday in Homicide.

But this time before Christmas, when the kids were out of school, people were occupied with baking cookies, shopping, gift wrapping, and going to Zoolights, the department was quiet and peaceful. They would pass the longest night of the year, and after Winter Solstice, the days would start to get longer again.

It was a good time to tie up loose ends and clear the decks for what was ahead.

On Friday, Christina wanted to spend some time with Tracy and his family. They were not Christian, but still enjoyed Christmas traditions of their own. With her daughter out of the house for the evening, Margie decided to take advantage of the opportunity to canvass Bowness Park for her witness. The woman would, presumably, follow the same routine every day, so she should be in the park at roughly the same time as she had been the night of Robertson's death.

While they had a good circumstantial case against Petrov, they didn't have proof that he had harmed Robertson. He might argue that he had wanted to meet with her, wanted her to publish his story, showing off the hard work of his Russian family and leaking some information about a rival family. He could claim that someone else had gotten to her or that a tragic accident had occurred.

Margie needed to find that witness.

Margie informed Christina that she would be doing a little work after hours but was still reachable on her phone. Christina wouldn't call. She would be watching a movie with Tracy and his parents, playing a game, decorating, or making cookies. Christina wouldn't worry about what her mother was up to.

⋅⋅⋅

THE AIR WAS CRISP. It wasn't too cold yet; Margie would be fine as long as she bundled up for the weather. But the wind was picking up a little and there were warnings of an impending snowfall. For the moment, there was only a light snow, pretty, a fine sprinkling of flakes.

If things didn't work out tonight, Margie could return the next day. The pathways would be cleared quickly by Bobcats once the snow stopped falling. Dog walkers needed a place to walk their dogs. They would, Margie was sure, make irritated calls to the city to have the pathways cleared if they were not done quickly enough.

Stella was excited to be in a new place, walking outside with her person. She sniffed everything and wanted to meet all the other dogs and people there. She was well-behaved and didn't try to jump up on anyone or strain on the leash as Margie tried to talk to the other dog owners before allowing the dogs to smell each other. Margie had figured that other dog walkers would be more accepting of a stranger's presence if she were there walking Stella than if she were a solitary walker stopping to talk to the dog walkers and asking questions about whether they had been there the night that Robertson had been killed.

But with Stella there to break the ice, the questions came naturally. Margie expressed concerns about the safety of walking in the park after that woman had fallen through the ice and drowned. She wanted assurances from people who had been there that night, and they were eager to oblige.

She knew the woman she was looking for, had studied her picture many times since she and Siever had reviewed the video footage and they had identified her as a person of interest. But Margie was only assuming from the woman's expression that she had seen something that night, that she was the anonymous witness who had called in and then chickened out. She could have been upset about something else. Their witness might be someone else. In fact, they might have several witnesses who had seen parts of what had happened, and cobbling together their stories would provide an overall picture.

So Margie kept asking questions. Who had been there? Had they known the dead woman? Had they seen what had happened or seen anything else weird that night? Stella made friends with the other dogs and Margie asked her litany of questions, gradually eliminating dog walkers who had not been there or who had been there but not seen anything.

It was dark, of course, full dark by six o'clock, so the walkers stayed close to the streetlights or used flashlights or headlamps as they navigated the park. Margie studied everyone's faces, looking for the woman who had been on camera.

The temperature dropped by a few degrees, the snowfall was getting heavier and the flakes bigger. Stella was enjoying the fluffy snow, dancing around and using her snout to toss the loose piles of snow into the air, biting at the snowflakes as they fell back toward the ground.

Margie knew she should probably turn around and head back to her car. Come back tomorrow or the next day after the snow had stopped. But tonight, Christina was occupied, and Margie didn't want to have to leave her alone in the evening later in the week, with Christmas close at hand and only a few nights for them to enjoy her school break together.

Margie saw the dog first. A shepherd cross, by the looks of him. Coming toward them. Margie thought he looked like the dog she had seen on the tape. She looked at the woman's face and, when she studied it, accounting for the scarf, she was pretty sure it was the woman who had been following Petrov out of the park. On her way home now, going back toward the parking lot.

Margie steered Stella closer to the shepherd and pretended to be lost in thought or absorbed by Stella's antics until they were only a few steps apart. Then she smiled at the woman and Stella pulled in the shepherd's direction.

"Is he friendly?"

"Yes, he'll be good."

They let the two dogs sniff and circle, getting to know each other.

"Do you come here regularly?" Margie asked.

"Yes, almost every night. Twice a day, if we can, but sometimes the morning gets a bit… frantic."

Margie recognized the woman's voice. She was definitely the person who had left the message on Margie's voicemail. She had seen what had happened out there on the ice.

Margie chuckled. "Oh, I hear you on that one. We go for a morning run if I can get up and get myself out the door, but it doesn't always work out."

"You don't run in this weather, do you?" the woman looked slightly alarmed at the thought.

Margie looked at the snow now falling thickly around them. "No, not like this. And not if the pathways haven't been cleared. Sometimes, it takes the city a couple of days to get them cleared."

"Yeah. They're pretty good about getting the main ones in the park done. But if there's a heavy snowfall for a few days, and then it doesn't get cleared for a few more days… it's disappointing. Harry doesn't understand why we can't come like usual."

Margie nodded. "Stella is the same way. She's very good about it, but she doesn't understand why she doesn't get to go for a run every day."

The woman started to move on, heading back toward the parking lot. Margie had been walking in the opposite direction, but now she looked at the increasing snowfall and decided to walk out with the woman, acting as though the incoming blizzard had changed her mind about the walk.

"It's really coming down," she observed. "Did you happen to be here when that woman fell through the ice?"

The witness looked at her, eyes widening. She looked around, wondering if it was an ambush. Which of course, it was, but not because Margie wanted to harm her or eliminate the witness, but because she needed to know what she had seen. If Margie were going to arrest Petrov, she needed more than just conjecture about what had happened.

"Who are you?" the woman demanded.

CHAPTER TWENTY-THREE

*M*argie didn't answer immediately. She studied the woman's face, trying to pick up every tiny indicator of expression.

"My name is Detective Patenaude," she said finally. "I am a homicide detective."

"Oh."

The woman's face was pale. Maybe it was just the cold or her natural pallor. But she looked scared, uncertain as to the correct course of action to take now. She wanted to run, but she also wanted to unburden herself. She probably had conflicting ideas about the right thing to do. Help the police, of course, help see justice served. But also to protect herself, her family, and her quality of life.

But she had witnessed something frightening. It was hard not to talk to someone about it, but it probably also felt unsafe. If the man knew who she was and knew she had talked, he might come after her next. And Margie knew that if the woman agreed to testify in court, her name would be revealed, compromising her safety. She might put the Russian in prison, but what about the rest of the organization? She couldn't put them all in prison.

"You called me," Margie said. "You saw what happened out there and were going to tell me what happened. Then you didn't leave your name or number. You didn't call back."

"I was afraid. I wasn't sure... what I should do."

"A woman is dead. Everybody is telling me that it was just an accident. But do you know what? I don't think it was. I don't think she just happened to walk out on the ice and fall in."

The witness snorted. "No. That's not how it happened."

"Then I need you to talk to me about it. Let's talk about what happened out there. What you saw. And then we can work on making sure you are safe."

"I don't know. It all happened so fast. It was nighttime; you see how dark it gets." She lifted her hands to indicate the world around them. Dark as pitch outside of the lights and flashlights. "Maybe I'm not sure what happened."

"What's your name?"

The woman hesitated. It was a big ask. But she had also grown up being taught to give her name when required. She had been taught to do what the cops told her to do. She wanted Margie to do something for her in return. To make her feel safe again. She couldn't ask for protection if she wouldn't even give her name.

"Lacey," she said eventually. "Lacey Brown."

"Well, Mrs. Brown, I appreciate you calling us to tell us something happened that night. There has been a lot of speculation, and it will be nice to talk to someone who saw something, who knows something concrete."

"I don't know what I saw."

"Let's talk about what you do know. Tell me about it, and then we can discuss whether you want to make a formal, written statement. We'll start with just talking."

"Okay." Lacey rubbed her chin, pushing her scarf around. Touching her face was a nervous gesture. Harry, her dog, bumped against her leg and whined. Lacey's hand dropped down and she scratched his ears, which calmed her.

"You were out here that night walking Harry. Who did you see first? The woman or the man?"

"The woman, I guess. I must have walked into the park behind her. I wasn't paying much attention at that point. She was a big woman, didn't move very fast. Harry always has to stop and sniff everything, so we weren't going anywhere very quickly either. A few times, she turned around to look at us or around the park. I thought she was looking for someone. The rest of the time, she was looking at her phone. It's dangerous to walk around a wild, dark place like this looking at your phone. It dazzles you, eliminates any night vision. If you're not watching where you are going, you could accidentally step off of the pathway or into a depression in the pathway and twist your ankle or fall." She looked rueful. "If anyone knows that, it's me!"

"We're all so dependent on our phones, I think anyone can relate. We've all done something stupid—walked into a newspaper box, accidentally stepped out into traffic without looking, or just stepped on the heel of the person walking in front of you."

Lacey nodded. She looked at Margie, uncertain about going on. Margie motioned for her to continue, not wanting to derail her description with any questions.

"So… I thought she was a little strange because I hadn't seen her here before and she spent the whole time looking at her phone. But, like I said, I figured she was here to meet someone. Getting directions or answering text messages. I just kept going with Harry on our usual route. Then, when we got toward the river… she left the pathway. I didn't know what to do."

"Did you call out to her?" Margie asked. "Warn her that the river was dangerous or that she should stay on the pathway?"

"No. I thought maybe I should, but it was obvious that she had a specific destination in mind, so she knew what she was doing. I didn't want to poke my nose into anything that wasn't my business, but I was worried about her, too. I didn't want someone unfamiliar with the area wandering in the dark. Even if she had directions, it's easy to get turned around in the dark or to misunderstand a direction."

Margie nodded her agreement. She was the master at getting lost and knew how easy it was to get lost even using a GPS with the roads highlighted on the screen right in front of her.

"So…" Lacey shifted uncomfortably and looked around. "We should keep moving; it's getting pretty fierce."

Margie had barely noticed the snow swirling around her, but it was getting heavy. Both dogs were gathering snow in their fur, and it was collecting on Lacey's hat and shoulders. Margie brushed and shook herself off, and they walked slowly toward the parking lot while continuing their conversation.

"I decided to follow her," Lacey admitted, finding it easier to talk while they walked side by side instead of looking Margie in the face. A lot of witnesses found too much eye contact uncomfortable even if they hadn't done anything wrong.

"She went out to the river?" Margie suggested. She wasn't worried about planting false memories with the suggestion. It was clear that Robertson had gone to the river. That was where she had died. Lacey had said she had seen what happened out on the ice that day.

"Yeah. I was a little nervous. I didn't want to get caught following her, but I didn't want to let her walk into danger if she didn't realize where she was going or couldn't see a danger in front of her. She just had the LED on her phone for a flashlight. Those lights aren't really strong, and it would run her battery down quickly."

Lacey looked around.

"It was a clear night, not like tonight. The sky was clear, so there was some light from the moon. She walked down to the river, and then I saw her boyfriend. Or whoever she was meeting for her assignation. I didn't know what kind of a meetup it was. She didn't hug him. They approached each other slowly, like they didn't know each other but had been set up to meet. Maybe it was a blind date or something; I didn't know for sure. The man had a dog. A black dog. Maybe a lab. So I figured he was a park regular, even though I didn't recognize him. They were a little distance away, so I couldn't see his face clearly. Maybe he usually walked there at a different time of the day, but he still knew his way around. I got ready to leave. Figured that they had met each other now and he knew his way around, so she would be safe."

Margie was disappointed. "Was that all that you saw, then?"

"No." Lacey cleared her throat. She scratched Harry's ears. They were out to the parking lot now, so there was more light and Margie could see the woman and her dog more clearly. Lacey turned away a little, still uncomfortable with direct eye contact. Still with more story to tell.

Margie nodded.

Lacey went on. "I was turning around to go when I heard raised voices. I couldn't tell what they were saying, but they certainly weren't lovers or on a blind date. I turned back and watched them, thinking that she might need help. I could do something if he turned... violent."

"That was very brave of you."

"I should have called 9-1-1. Gotten the police out there."

"Because two people raised their voices? I probably wouldn't have."

"No. But then... they were moving apart, but the man wouldn't let the woman return the way she had come. He kept moving in her way to block her. She had to keep retreating and going farther down the river, trying to find a way to get back to the pathway. I even left the pathway to get closer so that I could see."

"There was not much you could have done," Margie reassured her.

"No. I really wanted to. I wanted to help her. But... this guy was starting to get really aggressive. I could tell he was threatening her. I knew he was dangerous. But I was too involved. Frozen."

Petrov with ice in his veins. Lacey frozen where she was. And the ice crackling beneath Robertson's feet.

CHAPTER TWENTY-FOUR

*H*e shoved her and was yelling at her. She was trying to get away from him, backing toward the middle of the river. At the shore, you're safe. It's ice all the way down to the ground and perfectly stable. But the farther you get out, the thinner the ice is, and there is no land underneath it, just the river. And then." Lacey swallowed strenuously a few times. "Then he sicced the dog on her!"

Margie opened her mouth, but had nothing to say. Nothing that would make Lacey feel better. Nothing to ask. She just waited, holding her breath, for the rest of the story.

"The dog went after her, chased her across the ice. She was running as fast as she could. She was not in very good shape, but she was really moving. Trying to stay away from the dog. It was barking and snarling at her, snapping at her heels. She was screaming and flailing her purse at it. But she was running straight toward the middle of the river, where the water isn't even frozen. And she just… the shelf of ice that she was on cracked, and she went through it. I wanted to go out there and help her, but… she was so far away, and she was in the water, and I knew if I jumped in the water, I would never get back out. It paralyzes you when it's that cold. You can't move and you can't think, and you just go down and drown."

"I don't blame you. I don't see how you could have been expected to rescue her."

"And if I called 9-1-1… even if they got the river rescue out there, she would have been gone long before they could even find her."

"Yes." Margie knew the stats about drowning in freezing water. If someone wasn't right there to help—and often even if there was—the chances of survival were practically nil.

Lacey cleared her throat again. Harry was rubbing against her, still looking concerned. Margie was sure he knew his person was distressed and wanted to comfort her. "And then the man… he called his dog to him. They were turning around. I turned off my flashlight as fast as I could. I was too afraid that he would still be able to see me, so instead of going back to the pathway, I hid in some trees, where it was very dark. I stayed as still as I could. He never even looked in my direction. His dog did. The dog wanted to come and investigate and find out what I was doing there. But the man clipped the leash back on its collar to make sure that it stayed with him, and he wouldn't let it explore the bushes. He was quick to get back to the pathway and headed around the loop back to the parking lot."

"And after he was past you, you went the same way to the parking lot."

"It was the shortest way, I didn't want to go around the long way. I was pretty sure he hadn't seen me or realized he had been seen." Lacey looked down at the ground and petted Harry, taking a few shuddering breaths. "I read about that reporter in the news. And I called you… but I couldn't follow through. I was too afraid that if I revealed myself as a witness, he would come after me."

"We want to get this guy. I'll have you come down to the

office to look at some pictures so that you can identify him for me."

"I'm afraid…"

"We can't just let a killer go free. He lured her there and killed her, just as surely as if he had shot her. We don't have enough evidence without your testimony. All that we have is circumstantial evidence. A good theory. We need you to tell how it happened."

"He was… so menacing. I can't imagine having to look across the courtroom at him. He would know who I was, and I just can't.…"

Stella turned suddenly, growling. Margie whipped her head around to see what Stella had seen.

And he was there.

Victor Petrov.

He wasn't back in Winnipeg, where he should have been.

He was right there in Bowness Park.

Lacey gave a yelp and moved away. Harry stayed between the threat and his master, watching warily and growling. Stella was a smaller dog than Harry, and she barked and growled at the threat.

Not just Petrov, the ice-cold killer. But also his dog, a coal-black demon dog who stood there slavering and snarling.

"You were warned," he told Margie. He didn't spare a look at Lacey, who was melting down somewhere behind her now. She was crying and protesting that she didn't know anything and trying to put as much space between her and Margie as possible. Which was undoubtedly a good idea. Petrov had his target. He knew who the threat to his freedom was. And it wasn't Lacey, it was Margie.

Without Margie, nothing would ever come to fruition. The other detectives would deep-six the case, knowing that there were no more leads to follow up, no way to prove that it hadn't been an accident or suicide. They wouldn't find Lacey again.

Even if they did, she would not tell her story and would not testify against Petrov in court.

"You killed a woman," Margie told Petrov. She was trying to calculate her chances of survival. Could she get back to her car? Make a phone call? "Did you really think that I would drop the case?"

"You should have. A woman fell into the river and drowned. Why make such a big deal of that?"

His voice was higher than she had expected. A tenor rather than a bass. Not low and gravelly like a TV villain. But the killers she arrested were rarely like comic book or TV show killers. They were complex people. Most of whom confessed what they had done in the end. Many of them cried. Even the gang members tended not to be ice-cold killers. They were hotheaded, scared, drunk or high.

"Murder is murder," Margie told him, feeling for her phone in her pocket with clumsy, gloved hands. She would need to take off her gloves to call 9-1-1. And to see the screen. Unless...

"I can't just let it go," Margie said flatly.

"You could. Just like everyone else. I never laid a finger on her. How could it be murder?"

"We both know you took her life," Margie argued. "Right here in Bowness Park. Julia Louise Robertson never had a chance. Victor Petrov and his demon dog. How could anyone expect to stand up to you?"

"That's right," Victor agreed smugly, advancing toward Margie. "No one dares. No one does and survives."

"You make sure of that. You find a way to silence them. Just like Julia."

"Just like you," he corrected.

Margie stood her ground. He wasn't going to chase her into the river. She might not have a much better chance if he decided to pull a gun on her and shoot her at point-blank range. But people did survive gunshot wounds to the head or the heart. She wouldn't survive in the freezing cold water in the dark, with no one around.

She looked around, hoping to see crowds of dog walkers and fitness buffs out for their evening walks. But the storm had chased them away. The snow was swirling thickly around them. The wind was picking up. Snow was drifting along the edges of the pathways and curbs of the parking lot. The wind cut into Margie, even through her warm winter coat.

"Get her!" Petrov ordered his dog, which was not on leash, pointing at Margie. The black dog took a couple of bounds toward her, snarling like a demon. Stella released a volley of threatening barks and growls, baring her teeth and screaming like a banshee.

The black dog was stopped in its tracks. It slunk around, circling, trying to get around behind them for a better opportunity to attack. Margie turned, not allowing it to get behind her. If she kept turning, that would put Petrov behind her, so she stepped backward, trying to keep them both in sight and put more distance between herself and the two threats. Petrov still had not seen the need to draw a gun, but was shouting at the dog, berating it, trying to whip it into a frenzy so it would attack.

Margie talked to the dog in a quiet, calm voice, though she knew in her heart of hearts that there was no way she would be able to calm it down and counteract Petrov's orders. The dog knew who its master was. The dog had killed before. Multiple times, if Margie was right. She was sure that Robertson's death wasn't the first that the dog had been responsible for. And probably the other attacks had been more up-close and personal. Not everyone would obligingly fall into the icy river.

CHAPTER TWENTY-FIVE

*A*t first, Margie wasn't sure she could actually hear sirens over the noise of the wind and the barking, snarling dogs. She was listening for them, hoping, but not sure they would come.

Stella looked around. Petrov's demon dog finally managed to reach Margie as she looked down at Stella, both distracted by the sound. Both reacting instinctively to the sound of a siren.

The dog went first for the back of Margie's calf. Margie kicked out, trying to escape it and force it back at the same time. Stella screamed and snarled, her teeth ripping into the shoulder of the black dog when it moved in.

Margie tried to bar it with her arm when it jumped up at her on its next attempt. The dog's teeth sank into her puffy sleeve, finding more fiberfill than flesh. There was the sound of tearing fabric as the dog tried to rip at her. Stella struck again and the other dog yipped and whirled around, trying to defend itself as well as attacking its target.

The sirens got louder. There was no mistaking them now.

Petrov shouted for his dog, trying to call it back. He looked for the best avenue of escape. Into the darkness of the trees? To his car? There was a gun in his hand now; he wouldn't be going down without a fight.

The police cars rolled into the parking lot, sirens screaming. As much as Margie wanted to collapse or relax her focus, she fought to stay in control. She could not let down her guard until she knew that she and Stella and anyone else around them were safe.

A couple of shots were exchanged between Petrov and the arriving cops. Margie didn't even have her sidearm with her. She had come to the park to walk her dog and search for witnesses, not to fight a madman and his mad dog.

Petrov fled into the trees with his dog. The darkness and drifting snow swallowed him up. Several cops pursued, flashlights in hand. Margie didn't know if they would be able to catch up or find them in the inky darkness. It was a big park.

"Are you okay?" A couple of the responding officers approached Margie. They reached for her, held her steady as they walked her back to one of the cars to sit down.

"I'm fine," Margie insisted. "Fine, fine."

They ignored her, herding her back to safety. Sitting in one of the squad cars with her feet out the open door, Margie looked down at herself as they ministered to her. More sirens were audible, more police cars and an ambulance pulled into the parking lot.

"You should look for a woman with a dog," Margie said. "Her name is Lacey. She's a witness. I don't think she was hurt, but…"

"I think we've got her farther up the road," one of the officers assured her. "She made it to her car and called 9-1-1."

"So you got *her* call," Margie said.

"We got yours too. The emergency operators were able to

use both to get a clearer picture of what was going on and dispatch multiple units."

"I wasn't sure if mine went through. I've drilled on making emergency calls on my phone with just the hardware buttons. They tend to change the settings every time you update the operating system. I've never actually had to do it before."

"Well, it worked. Not the clearest call. Lots of background noise. But that, together with the second call, was enough."

Margie's heart was starting to slow. She pulled Stella against her, scratching her ears and petting her head, murmuring to her. "Good girl. Who's my good girl?"

She wanted to wipe the blood from Stella's muzzle, but didn't dare. The crime scene techs would want to swab her to take samples.

"Let's have a look at you, then," one of the cops said, pulling at Margie's sleeve. She had to unbutton her coat to get her arm out of the sleeve, and felt a chilling rush of air.

She was surprised to see a small amount of blood and puncture marks in her arm. She hadn't thought that the black dog had actually hurt her. She hadn't felt it. Still couldn't feel it. But she started to shake, a combination of the adrenaline rush and the cold air on her body.

The black-masked paramedics were allowed onto the scene, since the shooter was not in the immediate area. They looked at Margie's arm and bandaged it, but told her that she would need to have it looked at at the hospital and to have shots. They were initially nervous of Stella, blood on her muzzle, thinking that she was the one who had bitten Margie, but she assured them that Stella had only defended her, had only slashed another dog, not a human.

"She wouldn't ever hurt anyone, would you, Stella?" Margie asked Stella in her "good dog" voice.

"Detective Patenaude," a familiar voice intruded into the

conversation with the paramedics. "What have you gotten yourself into?"

Margie looked up and saw Detective Cruz, bundled up in a thick winter coat, a scarf wrapped around the lower part of his face.

"What are you doing here?"

"Well, I heard some action on the police scanner and it sounded... suspicious. A couple of calls confirmed that one of the members of my department was involved."

Margie's face warmed in embarrassment, but she was grateful to have someone familiar there with her. She was glad that he had come.

"Things went in an unexpected direction," she admitted.

"I guess so. What is this all about? What are you even doing on this side of town?"

"I was looking for a potential witness. The one who had called in anonymously. Siever and I found her on the surveillance tapes, and I was hoping she might walk her dog here regularly."

Cruz looked down at Stella and at Margie's bandaged arm. "And her dog attacked you? Are you suggesting that she was involved with Robertson's death, not just a witness?"

"No. No, this wasn't her..."

"Your own dog bit you?"

Margie shook her head emphatically. "Stella wouldn't hurt a fly. No, it was... Victor Petrov was here with his dog." She shuddered, remembering how it had looked at her. How he had sicced it on her after Margie had heard the story of how he had chased Robertson to the edge of the ice, causing her to fall in and drown in the frigid depths.

"Who?"

"Uh... Russian mob from Winnipeg. That's who Robertson was supposed to be meeting with. Nickname Iceberg."

"Encounter with Iceberg."

"Yes."

Cruz raised his brows, but didn't follow this up with another question about Petrov. Like how had Petrov known that Margie was going to be there? How had he just happened to be there at the same time as Margie? All of those questions that she couldn't answer.

"Are you okay?"

Margie nodded. "Fine. It's nothing. Very minor. It helps to be bundled up like a mummy." She looked down at her winter gear. "It's not that different from the body suits they wear while training police dogs in takedowns. He could hardly find my arm underneath all of the padding."

"That's lucky. What happened? Did you attempt an arrest?"

If Cruz had been listening to the police channel and had talked to whoever was in charge of the scene when he arrived, he probably knew more details about it than Margie did. But he was letting her tell her story in her own way.

"No… all I could do was call 9-1-1. I didn't come here expecting to find him. Wasn't armed. He just showed up out of nowhere. Then he rabbited when the cavalry arrived."

Cruz nodded. He looked off into the distance. Standing, he had a much better vantage point than Margie.

"Did they catch him?" she asked.

"Still working on it. They have a perimeter. But I don't know how secure it is. With all of the green space, there are a lot of places to hide. And there are probably a lot of places you can come out on foot that can't be blocked like the main roads. And if you don't know where he came from, it's even possible that he has a house in the area that he owns or stays at when he is in town. Maybe that's why he was here the night Robertson died."

"It was murder," Margie told him. "I found the witness."

"How?"

Margie explained it to him. Cruz pulled his coat tighter to him, shaking his head. "Hard to believe."

"It matches up with what is on the surveillance tapes."

&.

THINGS PROGRESSED SLOWLY, as they always seemed to. Crime scenes took time to process. Witnesses were interviewed and reinterviewed. It was cold, windy, and snowy, obliterating the crime scene. They did manage to get a couple of crime scene techs out to process a few footprints and the blood on Stella's muzzle. Coordinating the search for Petrov would take long hours and, not only was Margie not required to be part of it, she was barred from participating.

"I'll take you to the hospital," Cruz told her. "You should get that taken care of tonight."

"It's not that serious."

"Didn't they say it needed further treatment?"

"Well… yes."

"Then I'll take you to the hospital."

"I can drive myself."

"Not like this, you can't. You were attacked, and the adrenaline will probably have you all wobbly. Your brain is in fight or flight mode, not driving calmly and noticing all the hazards. And in case you didn't notice, we're in the middle of a blizzard."

Margie laughed. "Which means that the person from Winnipeg is probably a better bet for driving safely than the person from the Philippines."

"I'm qualified," he told her sternly. "I've lived here long enough to learn to drive in all weather conditions. Come on. Bring Stella, and we'll go in my car."

"What about my car?"

"We'll deal with that tomorrow. I'll bring you back, or we'll get one of the others to pick it up. But you're not in any shape to drive tonight."

"Jason Bourne always does his own driving."

"Not when he's been bitten by a dog and it's snowing."

They both laughed, and Margie conceded, letting Cruz take her back to his car. Stella was eager to get out of the storm and had no qualms about jumping into the back seat of a strange car when Margie opened the door for her.

CHAPTER TWENTY-SIX

There was a wait when Margie and Cruz got to the emergency room at the Lougheed Hospital. Apparently, even injured police officers had to follow proper triage protocols, and a non-life-threatening dog bite was well down the list in terms of urgency. Margie would have preferred to go home and seek further care the next day or in a couple of days when she could schedule an appointment at one of the medical clinics rather than dealing with the emergency room. But Cruz didn't give her that option.

While waiting at the hospital, she called Christina and explained that she'd gotten a dog bite while walking Stella.

Christina was bright enough to know that there was something more going on. "What were you doing walking her in a blizzard?"

"Well…" Margie tried to come up with a logical explanation that didn't involve telling Christina that she'd been working on a homicide investigation at the time.

"You were working," Christina accused.

"I was looking for a witness, who I figured would be out walking her dog."

"And her dog attacked you?"

"No. It was another dog. Do you want to just stay there with Tracy's family, and then I'll pick you up when I'm finished here?" Margie ignored the fact that she didn't have her car with her. Cruz would take her to pick up Christina. Or she could get a ride share if she could convince him to go home to his family.

"No, I'm coming there," Christina asserted. "Tracy can bring me."

❧

SOME TIME after Christina got there and was reassured that Margie did not have any serious injuries, Margie looked up from her bored scrolling on her phone to see Staff Sergeant MacDonald striding toward her, his long legs eating up the distance. She shifted to get to her feet, but Cruz pushed her shoulder down and MacDonald motioned for her to stay put. He sat down in one of the chairs facing hers.

"So, do you want to tell me exactly what happened in Bowness Park, Detective Patenaude?"

Margie explained as succinctly as she could, not trying to excuse herself. She had, after all, only been trying to follow up on a witness. That was her job.

"Didn't I tell you to let the Winnipeg connection go?" MacDonald asked.

"Yes, sir. This was a witness in Calgary. Someone who had called in to say that she had seen what had happened."

"I don't remember you telling me you had identified that potential witness. Exactly how did you do that?"

"I… I identified Petrov going in and out of the park and, when he left, she was behind him."

"So you *were* working on the Petrov connection."

"He was here in Calgary. He did kill Robertson."

She could see that he wanted to reiterate that she wasn't supposed to be following the Winnipeg connection. But she had found the killer, and what could he say about her investigating a line of questioning that was not, in fact, a dead end? Detectives didn't stop investigating certain lines of inquiry just because they were politically fraught.

"Why was Petrov at the park?" he asked instead. "Did he know that you were going to be there? How?"

"I don't know how. I thought I was pretty careful. I was worried about the possibility of leaks," Margie wasn't sure how to put this in a way that didn't indicate that there might be a police department mole, "so I was really careful. I didn't do any searches that would be logged on our systems."

"How do you do that? I thought any database record access was part of the audit log."

"Yeah. So I didn't do any police database searches. Only public search engines and commercial databases."

"On our computer network?"

"No… I used my daughter's computer," Margie confessed.

"Did you use it to log into our network?"

"No. Completely separate."

MacDonald shook his head. "Well, something you did must have tipped him off. Talk to Siever. Maybe he can figure out where the tripwire was."

"I'll talk to him," Margie agreed. Siever was the most likely one to be able to help her sort out technological issues. But she also worried that he was the only one who had known that she had found the witness and was going to question her, and that information had somehow made its way to Petrov.

It couldn't have been a coincidence that Petrov had just happened to be in the park.

CHAPTER TWENTY-SEVEN

By the time Margie had finally seen the doctor to get her wounds treated and rebandaged, as well as getting her first shots and the instructions for the protocol she should follow, the emergency room had quieted down quite a bit. Christina was still there, playing on her phone and waiting in the chairs, accompanied, not by Cruz or MacDonald, but by Detective Kaitlyn Jones. Stella lay at their feet and, when Margie approached, gave a bored sigh and eye roll.

"Yes, we can go," Margie told Stella. She smiled at Christina and Jones. "Sorry to be so long. You must be tired of sitting here."

"You can't control how long you wait in a hospital emergency room," Jones said with a philosophical shrug. "It's like stepping into a different world where time is suspended. Things just happen when they happen."

"You didn't have to come," Margie told Jones.

"What? My fellow officer was injured in the line of duty. Of course I had to come."

"It's just a bite. A few puncture marks."

"Can I see?" Christina asked.

Margie's arm was bandaged up so she could not, but Margie had taken a picture before the bandage was applied, and showed off a picture of her war wounds to Christina and Jones.

"That doesn't look too bad," Christina said tentatively.

"No, it really isn't. I've got a bruise where he bit the back of my calf, too, but he didn't break the skin there. And… I have to get shots."

"Rabies?" Jones asked.

Margie nodded. "Unless they find and test the dog. And I think to do the tests, they have to kill it and examine its brain. They said the protocol isn't as bad as it used to be. I'd rather just do it and not worry about them having to put the dog down."

"No," Christina agreed, covering Stella's ears. "You couldn't let them do that!"

Margie stretched her sore muscles. She had been tense for a long time, and the cold weather had not helped, nor had sitting in hard chairs and then having to be still, with her arm at an odd angle, while the doctor treated the punctures and put a couple of stitches across them.

"I don't suppose you've heard whether they caught him."

"The dog?" Jones asked, eyebrows up.

"Well… the dog too, I guess. But Petrov? Did they find him?"

Laughing, Jones nodded. "They got him. Footprints in the snow. It was coming down pretty good but, once they found fresh tracks, they were able to run him down."

"So he's in custody?" Margie checked.

"He'll probably be tucked into bed before you are."

Margie let out her breath. "Thank goodness!"

"They just booked him on assault of a peace officer today, but once you get all of the paperwork in and your witness corroboration, they'll charge him with the murder."

"So much for him being untouchable."

"We get them all, sooner or later."

"I hope so," Margie said. But she knew there was a small percentage that slipped through their fingers. With new DNA testing technology and genealogical tracing, they were getting some of the criminals who had escaped the net forty years ago. Still, Margie wasn't sure that putting a seventy-year-old in prison for the rest of his days was quite as satisfying as getting someone like Petrov within weeks of committing the crime. Now he would serve time for what he had done. Not enough, she was sure. The Canadian penal system was way too quick to let criminals back on the street again. But at least he would be away for a few years, unable to cause more havoc on Calgary's city streets.

"Now you can relax for Christmas," Christina said firmly. An order, rather than a request or suggestion.

Margie hid a smile and saluted. "Yes, ma'am."

EPILOGUE

*U*sually, Margie and Christina visited Moushoom at the care center. When the weather was nice and he was feeling good, they sometimes went for a walk from the home to the top of the irrigation canal that ran alongside Twenty-Sixth Street for some fresh air and a bit of nature, though the well-traveled strip of green space was far from being a wilderness area.

The weather had warmed rapidly in the early morning of the Twenty-Third, going from -17 Celsius to a balmy six degrees and, while it hadn't held there until Christmas, it was still a few degrees above freezing and refreshingly bright and clear.

Margie and Christina had gotten up early Christmas morning and taken stockings to the nursing home, where they had all opened their little gifts and recounted memories of Christmases past. After Moushoom had eaten his breakfast, they were allowed to take him out. It was a short drive to the house, and then, with Christina and Margie both standing close by to help if he had any problems, Moushoom was able to get up the three stairs to the front door and into the house.

There, he delighted in the Christmas tree decorated with some of his family's heirloom ornaments and a few new ones with Métis flags or symbols.

Moushoom gave the traditional Métis retelling of the Christmas story of Marie and Joseph and the birth of Emmanuel. He wasn't up to dancing jigs with Margie and Christina, but he clapped along to the music and whooped and laughed as he watched them. They all had the dinner Margie and Christina had prepared of bannock and fresh fish, then settled in front of the TV to watch *A Christmas Carol* and *It's a Wonderful Life*. Alexander, who had been married to Margie's cousin, and his son Quinn would join them later in the evening to do some crafts and have another go at the bannock and fish, and some wild game that Alexander had promised to bring.

Margie was thankful to have her family around her, and was at peace, knowing that Julia Louise Robertson's killer was behind bars and, for the moment, there were no burning cases on her desk.

It was the end of December, and those would come soon enough.

"*Gayayr Nwel,*" she murmured to Moushoom and Christina, both drowsing in front of the TV.

"*Gayayr Nwel,*" Moushoom repeated, rousing himself. "*On veut la paix sa terre.*"

Merry Christmas. May there be peace on earth.

BOWNESS PARK

In its early days, the park was a bustling recreational hub featuring a variety of attractions including a swimming pool, lagoon for canoeing and boating with musical accompaniment, a large dancing pavilion, a merry-go-round now housed in Calgary's Heritage Park, picnic areas, swings, teeter-totters, camping sites, and rentable cabins. From the 1920s to 1946, families often rented summer cottages there for retreats. However, many of these amenities gradually disappeared over time.

During the warmer months, visitors can enjoy paddle boating on the shallow lagoon, wading pools, boat rentals, and a children's train ride. The park is also equipped with numerous pathways, and firepits and BBQ stands, making it a popular spot for picnicking along the Bow River. In winter, Bowness Park transforms into a hub for outdoor skating on the lagoon.

The author recalls family reunions and church activities at the park, eating BBQ and playing in the playground and on the zip line. In her early years in Calgary, there was a small midway. In the winter months, she remembers skating, warming herself by the fires, and drinking hot chocolate.

Did you enjoy this book? Reviews and recommendations are vital to making a book successful.

Please leave a review at your favorite book store or review site and share it with your friends.

Don't miss the following bonus material:
Sign up for mailing list to get a free bonus
Read a sneak preview chapter
Other books by P.D. Workman
Learn more about the author

Get the Parks Pat Survival Pack!

Sign up for my newsletter and receive the **exclusive Parks Pat Survival Pack**, packed with bonus materials and extra goodies you won't find anywhere else.

Stay in the loop on new releases, special offers, and insider content—all delivered straight to your inbox.

Sign up today and start your adventure with Parks Pat!

https://shop.pdworkman.com/products/parks-pat-survival-pack

Here's what's inside:
• **Out with the Sunset (Book 1, eBook)**
Begin Margie's journey with her first gripping case as a Calgary homicide officer in the Parks Pat Mysteries.

- **Out with the Sunset (Book 1, Audiobook – Computer Narrated)**

Take the mystery on the go—perfect for your commute, workout, or a walk through the park.

- **Bonus Prequel Story: *Flight of the Bluejay***

Discover Margie's *true beginning*. Before she was a sleuth, she was a pregnant teen on the streets—fighting to survive and find her place in the world.

- **Discover Calgary's Treasures – Photo Minibook**

Step into the beauty of Calgary with this exclusive photo album showcasing the first 15 parks that inspired the series.

- **Digital Wallpapers**

Bring the beauty of Calgary's parks to your phone, tablet, or computer with stunning photography.

SNEAK PEEK AT GROUNDED
IN THE WIND

GROUNDED IN THE WIND

Perilous Heights, Hidden Depths

A stone's throw from Calgary's bustling airport lies Prairie Winds Park—a place of family fun hiding a deadly conspiracy.

When an illegal drone launch throws Calgary's skies into chaos, Detective Margie "Parks Pat" Patenaude follows the trail straight into danger. Beneath the drone's hum lies something far more sinister—a corpse in the park's tranquil scenery.

As she digs deeper, Margie uncovers a tangled web of cartel intrigue, escalating threats, and a plot that could cripple Calgary's infrastructure. Tension runs high within the homicide team, and the clock is ticking. To stop the next attack, Margie must rise above the turbulence and uncover the truth before the cartel strikes again.

Tropes you'll love:
1 Strong female detective
2 Cartel conspiracy

3 Police procedural with heart
4 Twisty, fast-paced mystery
5 Picturesque but deadly setting

Praise for the series:

⭐⭐⭐⭐⭐ "The writing is excellent, the plot is nice and twisty, and the characters and situations are believable. I'm looking forward to seeing where she takes these new characters."

⭐⭐⭐⭐⭐ "This is another well-written, briskly-paced mystery featuring great characters, lots of interesting glimpses into Canada's Indigenous culture, and a satisfying resolution— all wrapped up in a delightful quick-read police procedural."

Looking for a police procedural set in picturesque Canada? Let Award-winning and Bestselling Author P.D. Workman take you to her favourite Calgary parks, as Métis detective Margie Patenaude investigates murder in this fast-paced new series.

These short mysteries are just right for those days when you need a quick escape. Take a walk in a Calgary park with Parks Pat.

Soar into this gripping new installment today!

CHAPTER ONE

The day began like any other. Things had been pretty quiet on the homicide front, so the team had been working other Major Crimes cases, reviewing some cold homicides for any old evidence that might benefit from modern technology—such as more sophisticated search techniques, cutting-edge DNA testing, or an appeal to the public through social media. Margie looked forward to going home and spending some time with Christina at the end of the day. Her teenage daughter was getting older and more independent, and they didn't get nearly as much time together as Margie would have liked. Between Margie's work, Christina's school schedule, and Tracy, Christina's "friend who was a boy," it could be hard to connect for any meaningful length of time.

Margie had reached out lately to her cousins, now that more public gatherings were allowed, and was trying to arrange some extended family activities to reconnect them with some of the tribal "brothers" and "sisters" she had lost touch with since she had been Christina's age. She wanted to keep Christina connected with the Métis community, something that had not been easy during the early COVID months when they had first moved from Winnipeg to Calgary.

But tonight, they were planning a movie marathon, just Margie and Christina, bingeing Batman movies. Margie honestly wasn't that excited about the newest Batman, but was looking forward to some of the cheesier early TV episodes and movies.

Staff Sergeant MacDonald came out of his office and whistled to get everyone's attention, something she had never seen him do before. The effect was, therefore, instant. Everyone froze. Any banter between the detectives ceased, fingers froze over keyboards, and everyone looked at the tall, gray-haired man to see what was happening.

"We've got an incident," MacDonald announced. "A possible attack directed at the airport. A drone has been launched and has disrupted flights. The airport is locked down, all flights in and out have been suspended until the drone can be neutralized. Police all over the city are being scrambled to deal with the threat to public safety and ensure that the public does not panic. Messaging is that the source and intent of the drone are unknown, but there is no apparent danger to the public."

"*Is* there a danger?" Cruz asked.

"If there was going to be a weapons attack, it would likely have been deployed by now. It may be that the pilot lost control of the drone, it is being directed by someone without any real training or understanding of the restrictions they operate under, or that it is an act of mischief."

"Are they going to shoot it down?"

"They have methods to deal with it. Our job is to check out a potential launch area and see if we can locate the point it went up from and the pilot."

Margie's heart was pumping hard and fast. Even though it didn't sound like the drone was actually any threat, it was still very different from what they handled on a day-to-day basis and would unfold quickly. It was a dynamic situation that would require all of them to be at the top of their game to see that the public wasn't put at risk and didn't panic over nothing.

"Where are we going?" Kaitlyn Jones asked as everyone rose from their seats and quickly pulled on jackets, preparing to go.

"Prairie Winds Park is the apparent point of origin," MacDonald announced, "given the reported sightings."

Margie glanced around at the others, hoping they had a better idea of where Prairie Winds was than she did. She vaguely remembered it as a park the Calgary cousins had spoken of sledding at when they were all still kids. But Margie had rarely been to visit Calgary during the winter. When she had, they had found smaller hills close to home or gone skating at Bowness Park.

"I will send you all the GPS coordinates and you can use your maps apps if you are not familiar with it," MacDonald advised. "We will all be heading out at the same time and can probably travel as a convoy, but if you get separated we don't want anyone getting lost."

"You're going too?" Margie asked, surprised. MacDonald generally worked from the office and dealt with the mayor's office or other political situations rather than going to crime scenes.

"In this case, I think it is best that I be on site to deal with any communications issues immediately."

Margie nodded, as did the others, and they quickly prepared to leave. Margie's phone chirped, and she saw the GPS coordinates MacDonald had broadcast, underlined as a link that meant her phone recognized the data format and would open it in her maps app, as MacDonald had suggested.

"Do you want to go together?" Jones asked Margie.

Margie grimaced. Unfortunately, her poor sense of direction had become legendary in the department. Even with GPS directions, it would not be unusual for Margie to miss an exit or take a wrong turn and add an extra twenty minutes to the trip to a location that should have been easy to find. Margie was sure that neither the French explorers nor the Cree making up her Métis heritage would have been very impressed by her ability to navigate by map or by memory.

"What part of the city is it in?"

"Northeast. If you started at your house and went north up Fifty-Second—"

"Uh, right." Margie nodded. Considering the time and the fact that Jones would have to drive Margie back downtown to pick up her car after however long it took them to deal with the drone incident, Margie thought it was best not to impose on Jones. "I'd better take my car. Who knows how long this will take. We will probably be heading straight home afterward."

Jones nodded and pushed back a curled lock of blond hair that had escaped her bobby pins. "You're probably right. It shouldn't be too hard for you to get to, even if we get separated. We'll probably take Deerfoot, turn off at McKnight—"

"I'll just follow everyone else or the GPS," Margie interrupted. "There's no point in telling me the route ahead of time."

"You should just ride with someone else," Gagnon told her as he headed for the door. Though Margie noticed he did not offer to drive Margie as Jones had.

CHAPTER TWO

*W*ithin a few minutes, they were down to their cars and headed out in a convoy to the park.

No one had made any jokes about Detective "Parks Pat" being on this call. It was not her usual callout to a park because she had been specially requested by someone who thought she should be there to investigate a homicide in a park, since that was *her specialty*.

Not that Margie *had* any particular talent for solving murders that took place in parks. She couldn't track and was more likely to get lost than anyone else if she set off on a hiking trail alone.

She kept focused on Jones's car in front of her, following as closely as she could without putting herself in danger of rear-ending her at the speeds they were traveling. Deerfoot had a speed limit of 100 kilometers per hour, and escorted by patrol cars with flashing lights, they were quickly passing all other traffic. They would beat the 18 minutes predicted by her maps app.

Margie let her eyes stray to the sky once or twice, wondering whether she would be able to spot the drone or any military aircraft sent to take it down. Surely they wouldn't shoot it down over the city, even over an airport runway.

Would she even be able to see it? They hadn't been given any details on the size of the drone, whether it was a child's toy, the type that could deploy a missile, or something in between. She assumed it wasn't the missile type, if it had been launched from a park. But she couldn't imagine a child's toy causing a panic at the airport, either.

The other cars in the convoy were exiting, so Margie followed suit. At the speed they were driving, she probably would have missed the exit if she had been on her own. So much of the time, it seemed that her maps app did not inform her of an exit until she had passed it. It couldn't just be hers. Did everybody else experience the same thing, and they were just better at anticipating a turn or recovering from a wrong move? She didn't understand how she could be that much worse than anyone else when she was being directed by a computer. She also had the ability to make several wrong turns in a row trying to get back on track, while others recovered after the first one.

They had to slow down considerably to crawl through the curving, single-lane roads in a retail shopping area, so she figured she would be able to stay with the rest of the convoy without getting lost.

In a couple of minutes, they were pulling into the parking lot of Prairie Winds Park. They didn't take the time to find individual parking spots, but instead pulled onto the grass. Margie looked around. It didn't appear to be a large park. Not like Glenbow Ranch, Fish Creek, or Nose Hill. There was a splash park and some playground equipment. The big sledding hill was the central feature of the park, and Margie figured that was the most likely place to launch a drone. It had only a few trees at the top, with wide grass expanses encircling it. It was higher than anything else in the area. A good reason for the authorities to suspect this was where the drone had been launched from. MacDonald gave directions, sending his detectives around and up the hill from various directions. They would all converge at the top, having covered most of the park so they could report anything suspicious and work out a plan of action.

Margie and Detective Jones took the right-hand trail after walking through the playgrounds. They encouraged people to leave as they walked through, trying to make their warnings sound stern but not frightening enough to make people panic. "We are investigating a situation. We need people to return to their cars for their own safety. Please move along…"

More law enforcement officers would be arriving to help evacuate the park, so they didn't spend much precious time encouraging those who were resistant. They had a situation to investigate. Margie kept her eyes peeled for anything that might be a remote control for a drone, for any weapons, and for anyone who looked suspicious.

It wasn't the kind of situation where they could weed people out by whether they had children with them or not. There were plenty of people who went to the park alone, from athletes obviously training for their particular sports to seniors with walkers or hiking poles walking only the flat areas or the gentle slopes. Some children didn't seem to be attached to any of the adults present, but Margie figured that if anyone were to approach them and try to engage them or remove them, their parents would quickly make themselves known.

They walked along the pathway, heads on a swivel, checking 360 degrees around them for anything out of place or that might flag the launching point of the drone.

Margie had expected it to be pretty clear who was involved. She had thought the culprit would be showing off, making a big deal of what he had done, even if he knew it was illegal. But there was no launchpad that she could identify. No man or group of teens standing around a controller or staring up at the sky. Margie and Jones had worked small drones with cameras when they had been looking for evidence in Edworthy Park on a previous case, so she had some idea of what to look for.

"Have you seen anyone with a drone or controller?" they asked various people they encountered on the path, before directing them back to the parking lot.

"What is this?" demanded a dark-skinned man in a gray hoodie. "Where did you all come from, and what is this all about? I have a legitimate reason to be in the park; you can't just kick us out of a public place."

Margie looked him over. His racial origins weren't clear. He could be Hispanic or Indigenous, or a mix of any number of races. Was it possible he was Middle Eastern? Was it bad that her mind went there when they were investigating a potential terrorist act? His loose hoodie could be hiding weapons in his waistband or pockets. She didn't like the way he moved his hands as he talked or how confrontational he was.

"Sir, could I get you to put your hands on your head, please?" Margie instructed him in a steely cop voice, "Interlace your fingers."

"What?" he blustered, "You don't have any right to come around here and order me around. I'm not doing anything wrong, working out at a public park." He still gestured as he spoke.

"Hands on your head, now!" Jones ordered, her voice a shade louder than Margie's. They wanted to control him, but not cause concern or panic among the other park users. They didn't even know if he were anything to be concerned about at this point. They could be putting themselves at risk from another direction by focusing on an innocent bystander not accustomed to following orders.

The man's eyes widened and he tried to watch them both as

they approached him from different directions, each with their hands on their service weapons.

"Whoa, whoa, whoa," he said defensively, bringing his hands up to ear level and no longer gesticulating. "No need to overreact, here."

"Hands interlaced behind your head," Margie told him.

❧

Grounded in the Wind, Book #13 of the *Parks Pat Mysteries*
series by P.D. Workman
can be purchased at pdworkman.com or at your favorite online
retailer

❧

ABOUT THE AUTHOR

P.D. Workman is a USA Today Bestselling author and multi-award winner, renowned for her prolific output of over 100 published works that span various genres. With a knack for crafting page-turners, Workman captivates readers with everything from cozy mysteries like the Auntie Clem's Bakery series to gripping young adult and suspense novels.

A prolific reader and writer since childhood, P.D. Workman crafts emotionally powerful stories that don't shy away from hard topics. Her books tackle mental illness, addiction, abuse, and trauma with raw honesty and compassion, giving voice to the often unheard. If you crave authentic, character-driven page-turners that hit deep and stay with you long after the final page, you're in the right place.

With each new release, fans eagerly anticipate another thrilling blend of thought-provoking storytelling and relatable characters that define P.D. Workman's brand as an author of unforgettable page-turners—gripping tales that leave a lasting impact long after the last page is turned.

P. D. Workman, does not shy from probing the deep psychological scars of childhood trauma, mental illness, and addiction. Also characteristic of this author, these extremely sensitive issues are explored with extensive empathy, described with incredible clarity, and portrayed with profound insight.

Some of Workman's titles have been translated into Spanish, French, Portuguese, German, and Italian.

Workman began writing at an early age and is a prolific reader as well as writer. She is also passionate about teaching and learning, expresses her creativity through art and cooking, and loves exploring the Calgary parks and green spaces where the Parks Pat Mysteries are set. She was a legal assistant for many years and has done extensive charitable work.

Workman was born and raised in Alberta, Canada, and is married with one adult son.

❧

Please visit P.D. Workman at pdworkman.com to see what else she is working on, to join her mailing list, and to link to her social networks.

❧

If you enjoyed this book, please take the time to recommend it to other purchasers with a review or star rating and share it with your friends!

tiktok.com/@pdworkmanauthor

facebook.com/pdworkmanauthor

x.com/pdworkmanauthor

instagram.com/pdworkmanauthor

amazon.com/author/pdworkman

bookbub.com/authors/p-d-workman

goodreads.com/pdworkman

linkedin.com/in/pdworkman

pinterest.com/pdworkmanauthor

youtube.com/pdworkman

Find P.D. Workman's books at

PDWORKMAN.COM

Scan the QR code below